ILLUSTRATED CLASSICS

Alice in Wonderland

Lewis Carroll

Adapted by
Lucy Collins

Edited by
Claire Black

Published by

Berryland
Books
www.berrylandbooks.com

Alice in Wonderland

Lewis Carroll

First Published in 2006 • Copyright © Berryland Books 2006
ISBN 1-84577-094-3 • Printed in India

Contents

CHAPTER I

Down the Rabbit Hole

Alice was tired of sitting by her sister on the bank, and having nothing to do. Now and then, she peeped into the book her sister was reading. But she found that the book contained no pictures or conversations. 'And of what use is a book,' thought Alice, 'without pictures or conversation?'

So, Alice started wondering if she should

make a nice daisy chain, or whether getting up and picking daisies would be too much trouble. Suddenly, her thoughts were interrupted, when, out of nowhere a White Rabbit with pink eyes ran by her.

There was nothing extraordinary in that; nor did Alice find it strange when she heard the Rabbit say to itself, 'Oh dear! Oh dear!..... I shall be late!' (Although when Alice thought about it afterwards, it occurred to her that she should have been surprised at this.)

Then, something even stranger happened. The Rabbit actually took a watch out of its waistcoat-pocket, glanced at it, and then hurried on!

Seeing this, Alice was filled with tremendous curiosity. She had never before seen a rabbit with either a waistcoat pocket or a watch to take out of it! At once she jumped up and ran after it across the field. Fortunately, she was just in time to see the rabbit pop down a large rabbit-hole under the hedge. Immediately, Alice went down after it, never once considering how in the world she was to get out again!

The rabbit-hole went straight on like a tunnel for some way, and then dipped suddenly down. So suddenly, that Alice did not even have time to think about stopping herself, before she found herself falling down a very deep well.

Either the well was very deep, or Alice fell very slowly, for as she went down, she had plenty of time to look about her. She even had time to wonder what was going to happen next. She tried to look down, but it was too dark to see anything. So, she looked at the sides of the well, and noticed that they were filled with cupboards and book-shelves. Here and there, she saw maps and pictures hung upon pegs. Alice took down a jar from one of the shelves as she passed. It was labeled 'ORANGE MARMALADE'. But, to her great disappointment it was empty. Alice did not like to drop the jar, fearing that she might kill somebody. So, she managed to put it into another cupboard as she fell past it.

Down, down, down...

Alice kept falling. Would the fall never come to an end? 'I wonder how many miles I've fallen by this time?' she said loudly. 'By now I must be somewhere near the center of the earth!' Alice decided. 'I wonder if I shall fall right THROUGH the earth! How funny that would be!'

Down, down, down…

As there was nothing else to do, Alice soon began talking again. 'I think Dinah will miss me very much tonight!' (Dinah was her cat.) 'I hope they'll remember her saucer of milk at tea-time. Dinah my dear! How I wish you were down here with me!' Alice let out a big sigh. 'I am sorry that there are no mice in the air for you to catch. But you might catch a bat instead! A bat is so much like a mouse, you know. But do cats eat bats, I wonder?'

Here, Alice began to get rather sleepy and

went on saying to herself in a dreamy sort of way, 'Do CATS eat bats?' and sometimes, 'Do BATS eat cats?' You see, as Alice couldn't answer any of these questions, it didn't make much difference whichever way she put it.

Soon, Alice felt that she was dozing off. Alice even had a little dream that she and Dinah were walking hand in hand, and she was saying, 'Now, Dinah, tell me the truth - Did you ever eat a bat?' When suddenly, thump! Thump! Down fell Alice, upon a heap of sticks and dry leaves, and the fall was over.

Alice was not a bit hurt, and she jumped up and was on her feet in a moment. She looked up, but it was all dark. Before Alice was another long passage, and the White Rabbit was still in sight, hurrying down it. There was not a moment to be lost. Alice dashed after the Rabbit, and was just in time to hear it say, as it turned around the corner, 'Oh my ears and whiskers, it is getting very late!'

She was close behind it when she turned round the corner, but the Rabbit was no longer in sight. Alice found herself in a long and low ceiling hall. A row of lamps hanging from the roof lit up the hall. There were doors all around the hall, but all of them were locked.

Alice walked up and down the hall attempting to open each door as she went, but in vain. When she had tried every door, she walked down the middle of the hall, gloomily.

As Alice was thinking about how she would make her way out, she suddenly came upon a little three-legged glass table. There was nothing on the table, except a tiny golden key. 'This might belong to one of the doors of the hall!' thought Alice, hopefully. But, alas! Either the locks were too large, or the key was too small. In any case, no matter how hard she tried, the key would not open any of them. However, when she walked down the hall for the second time, Alice came upon a little curtain she had not noticed before. Behind it was a tiny door about fifteen inches high. Promptly, Alice tried the little golden key in the lock. And, to her great delight, it fit!

Alice opened the door and found that it led into a small passage, which was not much bigger than a rat-hole. She knelt down and looked along the passage. She found herself staring into the loveliest garden she had ever seen.

How Alice longed to get out of that dark hall! How much she wanted to walk about among those beds of bright flowers and those cool fountains! But, she could not even get her head through the doorway. 'And even if my head would go through,' thought poor Alice, 'it would be of very little use without my shoulders. Oh, how I wish I could shut up like a telescope! I think I could do that, if only I knew how to begin.'

You see, so many strange things had happened lately that Alice began to think that very few things indeed were really impossible. There was no use waiting by the little door, so Alice went back to the table. She was hoping that she might find another key on it, or maybe a book of rules for shutting people up like telescopes.

.However, this time she found a little bottle on it, (which was not there before) and round the neck of the bottle was a paper label, with the words 'DRINK ME' beautifully printed on it in large letters.

It was all very well to say 'Drink me.' But, wise little Alice was not going to take a chance.

'No, I'll look first,' she said, 'and see whether it is marked 'poison' or not.'

Alice had read several nice little histories about children who had got burnt, and eaten up by wild beasts and other unpleasant things, all because they would not remember the simple rules their friends had taught them. Rules, like - 'A red-hot poker will burn you if you hold it too long'; and that if you cut your finger very deeply with a knife, it usually bleeds. But the rule Alice had never forgotten was that, if you drink a large amount from a bottle marked 'poison,' sooner or later, you would surely find yourself in trouble.

However, this bottle was not marked 'poison.' So Alice ventured to taste it. She found it very nice (it had, in fact, a sort of mixed flavor of cherry-tart, custard, pineapple, roast turkey, toffee, and hot buttered toast). Very soon, she finished it off.

'What a curious feeling!' declared Alice; 'I must be shutting up like a telescope.'

And it was really so. She was now only ten inches high. She waited for a few minutes to see if she was going to shrink any further, feeling a little nervous.

After a while, finding that nothing more happened, Alice decided on going into the garden at once. But when she got to the door, she realized that she had forgotten the little golden key.

When Alice went back to the table for it, she found she was too small to reach it. Alice could see the key quite plainly through the glass, from where she was standing. She tried her best to climb up one of the legs of the table, but it was too slippery. When she was tired of trying, the poor little thing sat down and cried. 'Come, there's no use in crying like that!' said Alice to herself, rather sharply; 'I advise you to leave off this minute!'

Alice generally gave herself very good advice, (though she very seldom followed it). She remembered that once she had tried to box her own ears for having cheated herself in a game of croquet she was playing against herself. For this curious child was very fond of pretending to be two people. 'But it's no use now to pretend to be two people!' thought poor Alice, 'Why, there is hardly enough of me left to make even one respectable person!'

Soon, Alice saw a little glass box that was

lying under the table. She opened it, and found inside a very small cake on which the words 'EAT ME' were beautifully marked in currants. 'Well, I'll eat it,' said Alice, 'and if it makes me grow larger, I can reach the key. If it makes me grow smaller, I can creep under the door. So either way I will get into the garden, and I don't care which happens!'

Alice ate a little bit, and said anxiously to herself, 'Small or big? Small or big?' holding her hand on the top of her head to feel which way it was growing. She was quite surprised to find that she remained the same size!

Actually, this is what generally happens when one eats cake, but Alice had got so much used to expecting unusual things to happen, that it seemed quite dull and stupid for life to go on in the normal manner. Very soon, she finished off the cake.

CHAPTER 2

The Pool of Tears

'Curiouser and curiouser!' cried Alice, (she was so surprised, that for the moment she forgot to speak good English). 'Now I'm opening out like the largest telescope that ever was!' Then, as she looked down at her feet, she saw that they were getting so far off that they almost seemed to be out of sight.

'Good-bye, feet!' sighed Alice. 'Oh, my poor

little feet; I wonder who will put on your shoes and stockings for you now, dears? I'm sure I won't be able to do that, as I will be very far off. You must manage as best you can.'

Then, Alice thought, 'But I must be kind to them, or perhaps they won't walk the way I want to go! I think I will give them a new pair of boots every Christmas, to keep them happy.'

Alice then went on planning to herself how she would manage it. 'They must go by the post,' she thought; 'and how funny it'll seem, sending presents to one's own feet! And how odd will the directions look!

Alice's right foot, Esq.,
Hearthrug
Near the Fender,
With love,
Alice.

'Oh! What nonsense am I talking?!' Alice scolded herself.

Just then, her head struck against the roof of

the hall, as she was now more than nine feet high! She immediately grabbed the little golden key and hurried off to the garden door.

Poor Alice! All she could do was to lie down on one side, and look through into the garden with one eye, but to get past was more hopeless than ever. So she sat down crying, shedding gallons of tears, until there was a large pool of tears all round her.

After some time, Alice heard a pattering of feet. She quickly dried her eyes to see what was coming.

It was the White Rabbit returning, splendidly dressed, with a pair of white kid gloves in one hand, and a large fan in the other. He came trotting along in a great hurry, muttering, 'Oh! The Duchess, the Duchess! Oh! Won't she be savage if I've keep her waiting!' Alice felt so desperate that she was ready to ask for help from anyone. When the Rabbit came near her, she approached him in a low voice, ''If you please,

sir—"The Rabbit started violently, dropped the white kid gloves and the fan, and ran away into the darkness as fast as he could go.

Surprised, Alice took up the fan and gloves. It was very hot in the hall, so, she kept fanning herself and all the time she went on talking to herself.

Then, she looked down at her hands. To her surprise she found that she had put on one of the Rabbit's little white kid gloves! 'How could I have done that?' she thought. 'I must be growing small again.' Alice got up and went to the table to measure herself by it and found that she was now about two feet high. She soon found out that this was because of the fan she was holding. She dropped the fan hastily, just in time to avoid shrinking away altogether.

'That WAS a narrow escape!' exclaimed Alice, who was much frightened at this sudden change. But still she was glad to find herself still in existence; and now I shall go to the garden!'

Then, she ran to the little door. But, alas! The little door was shut again, and the key was lying on the glass table as before.

'And things are worse than ever,' thought the poor child, 'for I was never so small like this before. Never! And I declare it's too bad!' As she said these words her foot slipped, and in another moment, splash! She was up to her chin in salt water. Now, where had all this water come from?

Alice very soon realized that she was in the pool of tears which she had shed, when she was nine feet high. A few moments later, she heard something splashing about in the pool just a little distance away. So she swam nearer to make out what it was. At first, she thought that it must be a hippopotamus or a walrus. But when she remembered how small she was now, Alice was soon able to make out that the creature was only a mouse that had slipped in, just like she had.

'Would it be of any use, now,' thought Alice, 'to speak to this mouse? Everything is so different down here that I should think very likely it can talk. In any case, there's no harm in trying.'

So, Alice began, "O Mouse, do you know the way out of this pool? I am tired of swimming about here!" The Mouse said nothing. 'Perhaps it doesn't understand English,' thought Alice; 'I daresay it's a French mouse, which came over with William the Conqueror.' (You see, in spite of all her knowledge of history, Alice did not have the slightest idea about how long ago anything had happened!)

So she began again, "Ou est ma chatte?" (Where is my cat?) This was the first sentence in her French lesson-book. Hearing this, the Mouse gave a sudden leap out of the water, and seemed to quiver all over with fright.

"Oh, I beg your pardon!" cried Alice hastily, afraid that she had hurt the poor animal's feelings. "I quite forgot you didn't like cats." "Not like cats?!" shrieked the Mouse. "Would YOU like cats if you were me?"

"Well, perhaps not," said Alice in a soothing tone. "Don't be angry about it. And yet I wish I could show you our cat Dinah. I think you'd take a fancy to cats if you could only see her. She is such a dear thing," Alice went on, half to herself, as she swam lazily about in the pool, "and she sits purring so nicely by the fire, licking her paws and washing her face—and she is such a nice soft thing to nurse—and she's such an expert at catching mice…"

"Oh! Oh, I beg your pardon!" cried Alice again. For this time the Mouse was bristling all over, and she felt certain that the Mouse must be really offended.

"We won't talk about her any more if you don't like it."

"We indeed!" cried the Mouse, who was trembling down to the end of his tail. "Our family always HATED cats- nasty, low, vulgar things!

Don't let me hear the name again!"

"I won't indeed!" said Alice, who was now in a great hurry to change the subject of conversation. "Are you—are you fond—of—of dogs?"

The Mouse did not answer, so Alice went on eagerly, "There is such a nice little dog near our house I should like to show you! A little bright-eyed terrier, you know! And it'll fetch things when you throw them, and it'll sit up and beg for its dinner and do all sorts of things—I can't remember half of them. It belongs to a farmer, you know, and he says it's very useful. It's worth a hundred pounds! He says it kills all the rats and—oh dear!" cried Alice in a sorrowful tone, 'I'm afraid I've offended it again!'

For the Mouse was swimming away from her as hard as it could go, and making quite a commotion in the pool as it went.

So she called softly after it, "Mouse dear! Do come back again, and we won't talk about cats or dogs either, if you don't like them!" When the

Mouse heard this, it turned round and swam slowly back to her, its face was quite pale, and it said in a low trembling voice, "Let us get to the shore, and then I'll tell you my history, and you'll understand why I hate cats and dogs."

It was high time to go, for the pool was getting quite crowded with the birds and animals that had fallen into it. There was a Duck and a Dodo, a Lory and an Eaglet, and several other curious creatures. Alice led the way, and the whole party swam to the shore.

CHAPTER 3

A Caucus-Race and a Long Tale

They were indeed a queer-looking party that assembled on the bank – the birds with draggled feathers, the animals with their fur clinging close to them, and all dripping wet, cross, and uncomfortable.

The first question of course was how to get dry again. They had a consultation about this, and after a few minutes it seemed quite natural to Alice to find herself talking familiarly with them, as if she had known them all her life.

In fact, she had quite a long argument with the Lory, who at last turned sulky, and would only say, "I am older than you, and must know better."

However, Alice would not allow the Lory to be considered elder without knowing its age, and, as the Lory positively refused to tell its age, there was no more to be said.

At last the Mouse, who seemed to be a person of authority among them, called out, "Sit down, all of you, and listen to me! I'LL soon make you dry enough!"

They all sat down at once, in a large ring, with the Mouse in the middle. Alice kept her eyes anxiously fixed on the Mouse, for, she felt sure she would catch a bad cold if she did not get dry very soon.

"Ahem!" said the Mouse with an important air, "are you all ready? This is the driest thing I

know. Silence all round, if you please!

'William the Conqueror, whose cause was favored by the pope, was soon submitted to by the English, who wanted leaders, and had been of late much accustomed to usurpation and conquest.

Edwin and Morcar, the earls of Mercia and Northumbria—''

"Ugh!" said the Lory, with a shiver.

"I beg your pardon!" said the Mouse, frowning, but very politely. "Did you speak?"

"Not I!" said the Lory, hastily.

"I thought you did," said the Mouse. "—I proceed. 'Edwin and Morcar, the earls of Mercia and Northumbria, declared for him: and even Stigand, the patriotic archbishop of Canterbury, found it advisable—''

"Found WHAT?" asked the Duck. "Found IT," the Mouse replied rather crossly, "of course you know what 'it' means."

"I know what 'it' means well enough, when I

find a thing," said the Duck. "It's generally a frog or a worm. The question is — What did the arch-bishop find?"

The Mouse did not notice this question, but hurriedly went on,'— found it advisable to go with Edgar Atheling to meet William and offer him the crown. William's conduct at first was moderate. But the disrespect of his Normans—'

"How are you getting on now, my dear?" the Mouse continued, turning to Alice as it spoke.

"As wet as ever," said Alice in a melancholy tone, "it doesn't seem to dry me at all."

"In that case," said the Dodo solemnly, rising to its feet, "the meeting is over. And now, we should adopt more energetic remedies—"

"Speak English!" said the Eaglet. "I don't know the meaning of half of those long words, and, what's more, I don't believe you do either!" And the Eaglet bent down its head to hide a smile; some of the other birds too tittered audibly.

"I think," said the Dodo in an offended tone, "that the best thing to get us dry would be a Caucus-race."

"What IS a Caucus-race?" said Alice; not that she was much interested to know, but the Dodo had paused as if it thought that SOME-BODY ought to speak, and no one else seemed inclined to say anything.

"Why," said the Dodo, "the best way to explain it is to do it." First it marked out a race-course, in a sort of circle, ("the exact shape doesn't matter," it said,) and then all the party were placed along the course, here and there.

There was no 'One, two, three, and away,' but they began running when they liked, and halted when they liked, so that it was not easy to know when the race was over.

However, after almost half an hour or so of running, they were quite dry again; the Dodo suddenly called out, "The race is over!"

All the creatures crowded round it, panting,

and asking, "But who has won?"

The Dodo took a considerably long time to answer this question. It sat for a long time with one finger pressed upon its forehead (the position in which you usually see Shakespeare, in the pictures of him), while the rest waited in silence. At last the Dodo said, "EVERYBODY has won, and all must have prizes."

"But who is to give the prizes?" quite a chorus of voices asked. "Why, SHE, of course," said the Dodo, pointing to Alice with one finger; and the whole party at once crowded round her, calling out in a confused way, "Prizes! Prizes!"

Alice had no idea what to do, and in despair she put her hand in her pocket, and pulled out a box of candies, (luckily the salt water had not got into the box), and handed them round as prizes. There was exactly one piece for each one of them.

"But she must have a prize herself, you know," said the Mouse. "Of course," the Dodo replied very gravely. "What else have you got in your pocket?" he went on, turning to Alice.

"Only a thimble," said Alice, sadly. "Hand it over here," said the Dodo. Then they all crowded round her once more, while the Dodo solemnly presented the thimble, saying, "We beg your acceptance of this elegant thimble."

When the Dodo had finished this short speech, they all cheered. Alice thought the whole thing very absurd, but they all looked so grave that she did not dare to laugh. She could not think of anything to say, so, she simply bowed, and took the thimble, looking as solemn as she could.

The next thing was to eat the candies. This caused some noise and confusion. The large birds complained that they could not taste theirs; the small ones choked and had to be patted on the back.

However, it was over at last, and they sat down again in a ring, and begged the Mouse to tell them something more. "You promised to tell me your history," said Alice, "and the reason why you hate—C and D," she added in a whisper, half afraid that it would be offended again.

"Mine is a long and a sad tale!" said the Mouse, turning to Alice, and sighing.

"It is a long tail, certainly," said Alice, looking down with wonder at the Mouse's tail, "but, why do you call it sad?" And she kept on puzzling about it while the Mouse was speaking, so that her idea of the tale was something like this:—
We lived beneath the mat
 Warm and snug and fat
  But one woe, & that
   Was the cat!
   To our joys
   a clog, In
   our eyes a
  fog, On our
  hearts a log
 Was the dog!

When the
  cat's away,
   Then
    the mice
     will play,
      But, alas!
        one day (so they said)
          Came the dog and
            cat, Hunting
             for a rat,
              Crushed
               the mice
                all flat,
               Each
                one
                 as
                he
               sat
                Underneath the mat,
                 —warm, & snug, & fat...
                    'Think of that!'

Furry said
    to a
        mouse,
            That he
            met in the
            house,
        'Let us
    both go to
        law: I will
                prosecute
                YOU – Come,
            I'll take no
            denial: We
        must have a
    trial, For
really this morning
'I've nothing to do'
    said the
        mouse to the
            cur, "Such
            a trial,

dear Sir,
 With
   no jury
     or judge,
       Would be
         wasting
          our breath."
       "I'll be
       judge, I'll be
      the jury,"
     said
     cunning
   old Furry:
   "I'll
     try the
       whole
         cause,
           And
         condemn
           you
             to death."

"You are not attending!" said the Mouse to Alice, severely. "What are you thinking of?"

"I beg your pardon," said Alice very humbly, "you had got to the fifth bend, I think?"

"I had NOT!" cried the Mouse, sharply and very angrily. "A knot!" said Alice, always ready to present herself as useful and looking anxiously about her. "Oh, do let me help to undo it!"

"I shall do nothing of the sort," said the Mouse, getting up and walking away. "You insult me by talking such nonsense!"

"I didn't mean it!" pleaded poor Alice. "But you're so easily offended, you know!" The Mouse only growled in reply.

"Please come back and finish your story!" Alice called after it. All the others joined in chorus, "Yes, please do!" But, the Mouse only shook its head impatiently, and walked a little quicker.

"What a pity it wouldn't stay!" The Lory sighed, as soon as it was quite out of sight. Amongst all this, an old Crab seized the opportunity of saying to her daughter, "Ah, my dear! Let this be a lesson to you never to lose YOUR temper!"

"I wish I had our Dinah here!" said Alice aloud, addressing nobody in particular. "She'd soon fetch it back!"

"And who is Dinah, if I might ask?" said the Lory. Alice replied eagerly, for she was always ready to talk about her pet, "Dinah's our cat. You can't imagine what an expert she is, at catching mice! And oh, I wish you could see her after the birds! She'll eat a little bird as soon as she looks at it!" This speech caused a remarkable sensation among the party.

Some of the birds hurried off at once. The old Magpie began wrapping itself up very carefully, remarking, "I really must be getting home; the night-air doesn't suit my throat!" A Canary called out in a trembling voice to its children, "Come away, my dears! It's high time you were all in bed!"

On various pretexts they all moved off, and Alice was soon left alone. 'I wish I hadn't mentioned Dinah!' she said to herself, gloomily.

'Nobody seems to like her down here and I'm sure she's the best cat in the world! Oh, my dear Dinah! I wonder if I shall ever see you again!'

Now, poor Alice began to cry again, as she felt very lonely and low-spirited. In a little while, however, she again heard a little pattering of footsteps at a distance. Alice looked up eagerly, half hoping that the Mouse had changed his mind, and was coming back to finish his story.

CHAPTER 4

The Rabbit Sends in a Little Bill

It was the White Rabbit, trotting slowly back again, and looking anxiously about as it went, as if it had lost something. Alice heard it muttering to itself, 'The Duchess! The Duchess! Oh my dear paws!

Oh my fur and whiskers! She'll surely get me executed! Where CAN I have dropped them, I wonder?'

Alice guessed in a moment that it was looking for the fan and the pair of white kid gloves. So, she very good-naturedly began hunting about for them, but they were nowhere to be seen.

Everything seemed to have changed since her swim in the pool. The great hall with the glass table and the little door had vanished completely.

Very soon the Rabbit noticed Alice, as she went hunting about, and called out to her in an angry tone, "Why, Mary Ann, what ARE you doing out here? Run home this moment, and fetch me a pair of gloves and a fan! Be quick!"

And Alice was so much frightened that she ran off at once in the direction it pointed to, without trying to explain the mistake it had made.

'He took me for his housemaid,' she said to herself, as she ran. 'How surprised he'll be when he finds out who I am! But I'd better take him his fan and gloves--that is, if I can find them.'

As she said this, she came upon a neat little house. There was a bright brass plate on the door, with the name 'W. RABBIT' engraved upon it. Alice went in without knocking, and hurried upstairs, fearing that if she ran into the real Mary Ann, she would be turned out of the house before she had found the fan and gloves.

'How odd it seems,' Alice said to herself, 'to be running errands for a rabbit! I suppose Dinah will be the next one to make me work for her!'

And Alice began fancying the sort of thing that would happen: "Miss Alice! Come here directly, and get ready for your walk!" (Dinah would order her). "Coming in a minute, nurse!" (Alice would reply) "But I've got to see that the mouse doesn't get out."

'However, I don't think,' Alice went on, 'that they would let Dinah stay in the house if it began ordering people about like that!'

By this time Alice had found her way into a tidy little room with a table in the window, and on it (as she had hoped) a fan and two or three pairs of tiny white kid gloves.

Alice took up the fan and a pair of the gloves, and was just going to leave the room, when she saw a little bottle that stood near the looking-glass. There was no label this time with the words 'DRINK ME.' Nevertheless, she uncorked it and put it to her lips. 'I know SOMETHING interesting is sure to happen,' she said to herself, 'whenever I eat or drink anything; so I'll just see what this bottle does. I do hope it'll make me grow large again, for really I'm quite tired of being such a tiny little thing!'

It did so indeed, and much sooner than she had expected. For, before she had drunk half the bottle, she found her head pressing against the ceiling, and she had to stoop to save her neck from being broken.

Alice hastily put down the bottle, saying to herself, 'That's quite enough. I hope I shall not grow any more. As it is, I can't get out at the door. I wish I hadn't drunk quite so much!'

Alas! It was too late to wish that! She went on

growing, and growing, and very soon had to kneel down on the floor. In another minute there was not even room for this, and she tried the effect of lying down with one elbow against the door, and the other arm curled round her head.

Still Alice went on growing. As a last resource, she put one arm out of the window, and one foot up the chimney.

'I can't do anything more now,' she said to herself, 'whatever happens. What WILL become of me?'

Luckily for Alice, the little magic bottle had now had its full effect, and she grew no larger. Still it was very uncomfortable. Moreover, as there seemed to be no possibility of her ever getting out of the room again, she felt unhappy.

'It was much pleasanter at home,' thought poor Alice, 'when one wasn't always growing larger and smaller, and being ordered about by mice and rabbits. I almost wish I hadn't gone down that rabbit-hole—and yet—and yet—it's rather curious, you know, this sort of life! I do wonder what CAN have happened to me! When I used to read fairy-tales, I fancied that kind of thing never happened, and now here I am, right in the middle of one! There ought to be a book written about me! And when I grow up, I'll write one; but,' she added in a sorrowful tone, 'I'm grown up now!

At least there's no room to grow up any more HERE. But then,' thought Alice, 'shall I NEVER get any older than I am now? That'll be a comfort, one way—never to be an old woman—but then—always to have lessons to learn! Oh, I shouldn't like THAT!'

'Oh, you foolish Alice!' she answered herself. 'How can you learn lessons in here? Why, there's hardly room for YOU, and no room at all for any lesson-books!'

And so she went on, taking first one side and then the other, and making quite a conversation of it altogether. After a few minutes she heard a voice outside, and stopped to listen.

"Mary Ann! Mary Ann!" said the voice. "Fetch

me my gloves this moment!"

Then, she heard a little pattering of feet on the stairs. Alice knew it was the Rabbit coming to look for her, and she trembled till she shook the house, quite forgetting that she was now about a thousand times as large as the Rabbit, and had no reason to be afraid.

Presently the Rabbit came up to the door, and tried to open it. But, as the door opened inwards, and Alice's elbow was pressed hard against it, that attempt proved a failure. Alice heard the Rabbit say to itself, 'Then I'll go round and get in at the window.'

'THAT you won't!' thought Alice. Then, after waiting for a while till she fancied that she heard the Rabbit just under the window, Alice spread out her hand, and made a snatch in the air. Alice did not get hold of anything, but she heard a little shriek and a fall and a crash. 'The Rabbit must have crashed into something,' concluded Alice.

She waited for some time without hearing

anything more. At last came a rumbling of little cartwheels, and the sound of a good many voices all talking together.

Alice could make out the following words: "Where's the other ladder?—Why, I had to bring only one; Bill's got the other —Bill! Fetch it here! Here, Bill! Catch hold of this rope – Will the roof bear? – Mind that loose slate – Oh, it's coming down!

Mind your heads!' (A loud crash) – Now, who did that? – It was Bill, I fancy– Who's to go down the chimney? – No, I shall not! YOU do it! – That I won't, then! – Bill's to go down – Here, Bill! The master says you're to go down the chimney!''

'Oh! So Bill's got to come down the chimney, has he?' said Alice to herself. 'I wouldn't exchange places with Bill for the world. This fireplace is narrow, to be sure; but I THINK I can kick a little!'

Alice drew her foot as far down the chimney as she could, and waited till she heard a little animal (she couldn't guess of what sort it was) scratching and scrambling about in the chimney close above her. Then, saying to herself `This is Bill,' she gave one sharp kick, and waited to see what would happen next.

The first thing Alice heard was a general chorus of "There goes Bill!" Then, she heard the Rabbit saying—"Catch him!" then silence, and then another confusion of voices—"Hold up his head—

Don't choke him—How was it, old fellow? What happened to you? Tell us all about it!"

Last came a little feeble, squeaking voice, ('That's Bill,' thought Alice,) "Well, I hardly know—No more, thank you. I'm better now— but I'm very confused. All I know is that something came at me like a Jack-in-the-box, and I went flying in the air like a sky-rocket!"

"So you did!" said the others. "We must burn down the house!" said the Rabbit's voice.

At once Alice called out as loud as she could, "If you do, I'll set Dinah at you!" There was a dead silence instantly, and Alice thought to herself, 'I wonder what they WILL do next! If they had any sense, they'd take the roof off.'

After a minute or two, they began moving about again, and Alice heard the Rabbit say, 'A barrowful will do, to begin with.'

'A barrowful of WHAT?' thought Alice. And the very next moment a shower of little pebbles came rattling in at the window. Some of them even hit her in the face! 'I'll put a stop to this,' she said to herself, and shouted out, "You'd better not do that again!" which produced another dead silence.

Alice noticed with some surprise that the pebbles were all turning into little cakes as they lay on the floor. A bright idea struck Alice.

'If I eat one of these cakes,' she thought, 'it will surely make SOME change in my size; and as it can't possibly make me larger, it must make me smaller, I suppose.' So, she swallowed one of the cakes, and was delighted to find that she began shrinking instantly.

As soon as she was small enough to get through the door, she ran out of the house, and found quite a crowd of little animals and birds waiting outside.

The poor little Lizard, Bill, was in the middle, being held up by two guinea-pigs, who were giving it something out of a bottle. They all made a rush at Alice the moment she appeared.

But Alice ran off as hard as she could, and soon found herself safe in a thick wood.

'The first thing I've got to do,' said Alice to herself, as she wandered about in the wood, 'is to grow to my right size again; and the second thing is to find my way into that lovely garden. I think that will be the best plan.'

It sounded an excellent plan, no doubt. However, the only difficulty was that Alice did not have the faintest idea how to go about it. While she was looking about anxiously among the trees, a little sharp bark just over her head made her look up in a great hurry.

An enormous puppy was looking down at her with large round eyes, and was feebly stretching out one paw, trying to touch her.

'Poor little thing!' said Alice, in a coaxing tone, and she tried hard to whistle to it. But all the time Alice was terribly frightened; she was afraid that the puppy might be hungry, and might eat her up in spite of all her coaxing.

Hardly knowing what she did, Alice picked up a little bit of stick, and held it out to the puppy. The puppy jumped into the air, with a yelp of delight, and rushed at the stick. Then Alice dodged behind a great thistle, to keep herself from being run over. The moment Alice appeared on the other side, the puppy made another rush at the stick, and tumbled head over heels in its hurry to get hold of it.

Then Alice, thinking that this was much like having a game of play with a cart-horse, and expecting every moment to be trampled under its feet, ran round the thistle again. The puppy began

a series of short charges at the stick, and was bark-
ing aloud all the while.

And at last it sat down a good way off, panting, with its tongue hanging out of its mouth, and its
great eyes half shut.

Now Alice found a good opportunity to
escape. So, she set off at once, and ran till she was
quite tired and out of breath, and till the puppy's
bark sounded quite faint in the distance.

'And yet what a dear little puppy it was!' said
Alice, as she leant against a buttercup to rest herself, and fanned herself with one of the leaves. 'I
should have liked teaching it tricks very much, if–if
only I had been the right size to do so! Oh dear!
I'd nearly forgotten that I've got to grow up again!
Let me see, how IS it to be managed? I suppose I
ought to eat or drink something or other. But the
great question is WHAT?'

The great question certainly was WHAT? Alice
looked all round her at the flowers and the blades
of grass. But she could not find anything that

looked like the right thing to eat or drink.

She spotted a large mushroom growing near her, which was about the same height as her. She looked under it, and on both sides of it, and behind it. Then it occurred to her that she might as well look and see what was on the top of it. So, Alice stretched herself up on tiptoe, and peeped over the edge of the mushroom. Her eyes immediately met those of a large blue caterpillar that was sitting on the top with its arms folded, quietly smoking a long hookah. It did not take the smallest notice of Alice.

CHAPTER 5

Advice from a Caterpillar

The Caterpillar and Alice looked at each other for some time in silence. At last, the Caterpillar took the hookah out of its mouth, and addressed Alice in a sleepy voice.

"Who are YOU?" asked the Caterpillar.

This was not an encouraging conversation to begin with. Alice replied, rather shyly, "I--I hardly know, sir, just at present-- at least I know who I WAS when I got up this morning, but I think I must have been changed several times since then."

"What do you mean by that?" asked the Caterpillar, sternly. "Explain yourself!"

"I can't explain MYSELF, I'm afraid, sir," said Alice, "because I'm not myself, you see."

"I don't see," said the Caterpillar.

"I'm afraid I can't put it more clearly," Alice replied very politely, "or I can't understand it myself to begin with; and being so many different sizes in a day is very confusing."

"It isn't," said the Caterpillar.

"Well, perhaps you haven't found it so yet," said Alice; "but when you have to turn into a cocoon – which you will some day, you know – and then after that into a butterfly, I think you'll feel it a little queer, won't you?"

"Not a bit," said the Caterpillar.

"Well, perhaps your feelings may be different," said Alice; "all I know is it would feel very queer to ME." "You!" said the Caterpillar, contemptuously. "Who are YOU?" This question brought them back again to the beginning of the conversation.

"I think you ought to tell me who YOU are, first," said Alice, gravely.

"Why?" said the Caterpillar.

Here was another puzzling question. And as Alice could not think of any good reason, and as the Caterpillar seemed to be in a VERY unpleasant state of mind, she turned away.

"Come back!" the Caterpillar called after her. "I've something important to say!"

This sounded promising, certainly. So, Alice turned and came back again.

"Keep your temper," said the Caterpillar.

"Is that all?" said Alice, swallowing down her anger as well as she could.

"No," said the Caterpillar.

Alice thought she might as well wait, as she

had nothing else to do, and perhaps after all, the Caterpillar might tell her something worth hearing.

For a few minutes the Caterpillar puffed away without speaking. But at last it unfolded its arms, took the hookah out of its mouth again, and said, "So you think you're changed, do you?"

"I'm afraid I am, sir," said Alice; "I can't remember things as I used-- and I don't keep the same size for ten minutes together!"

"What size do you want to be?" the Caterpillar asked. "Oh, I'm not particular as to size," Alice hastily replied; "only one doesn't like changing so often, you know."

"I DON'T know," said the Caterpillar.

Alice said nothing. She had never been so much contradicted in her life before, and she felt that she was losing her temper.

"Are you content with your size right now?" asked the Caterpillar. "Well, I should like to be a LITTLE larger, sir, if you wouldn't mind," said

Alice. "Three inches is such a wretched height to be."

"It is a very good height indeed!" said the Caterpillar, angrily, rearing itself upright as it spoke (it was exactly three inches high).

"But I'm not used to it!" pleaded poor Alice, in a piteous tone. And she thought to herself, 'I wish the creatures wouldn't be so easily offend-ed.'

"You'll get used to it in time," said the Caterpillar; and it put the hookah into its mouth and began smoking again.

This time Alice waited patiently until it chose to speak again. In a minute or two, the Caterpillar took the hookah out of its mouth and yawned once or twice, and shook itself. Then it got down off the mushroom, and crawled away in the grass, merely remarking as it went, "One side will make you grow taller, and the other side will make you grow shorter."

'One side of WHAT? The other side of

WHAT?' thought Alice to herself.

"Of the mushroom," said the Caterpillar, as if Alice had asked it aloud; and in another moment it was out of sight!

Alice stretched her arms round the mushroom as far as they would go and broke off a bit of the edge with each hand.

'And now which is which?' she said to herself, and nibbled a little of the right-hand bit to try the effect.

The next moment, Alice felt a violent blow underneath her chin. Her chin had struck her foot!

Alice was a good deal frightened by this very sudden change, but she felt that there was no time to be lost, as she was shrinking rapidly. So, at once she began to eat some of the other bit. Her chin was pressed so closely against her foot, that there was hardly room to open her mouth. But, at last, she managed to swallow a morsel of the left-hand bit.

'Come, my head's free at last!' said Alice, delightedly. But the delight did not last long, as, soon Alice found that her shoulders were nowhere to be found! All she could see when she looked down was an immense length of neck, which seemed to rise like a stalk out of a sea of green leaves that lay far below her.

'What CAN all that green stuff be?' cried Alice. 'And where HAVE my shoulders got to? And oh, my poor hands, how is it I can't see you?'

She was moving them about as she spoke, but no result seemed to follow, except a little shaking among the distant green leaves.

As there seemed to be no chance of getting her hands up to her head Alice tried to get her head down to them. Alice was delighted to find that her neck would bend about easily in any direction, like a serpent.

Alice was about to dive in among the leaves, which she discovered to be nothing but the tops of the trees, when a loud hiss made her draw back in a hurry. A large pigeon had flown into her face, and was beating her violently with its wings.

"Serpent!" screamed the Pigeon.

"I'm NOT a serpent!" said Alice, indignantly. "Let me alone!"

"Serpent, I say again!" repeated the Pigeon, adding with a sort of sob.

"I've tried every way, and nothing seems to suit them!"

"I haven't the least idea what you're talking about," said Alice.

"I've tried the roots of trees, and I've tried banks, and I've tried hedges," the Pigeon went on, without paying her any heed; "but those ser-pents! There's no pleasing them!"

Alice was more and more puzzled, but she thought there was no use in saying anything till the Pigeon had finished.

"I must be on the look-out for serpents

night and day! Why, I haven't had a wink of sleep these three weeks!"

"I'm very sorry you've been annoyed," said Alice, who was beginning to see its meaning.

"And just as I'd taken the highest tree in the wood," continued the Pigeon, raising its voice to a shriek, "and just as I was thinking I should be free of them at last, one comes wriggling down from the sky! Ugh, Serpent!"

"But I'm NOT a serpent, I tell you!" said Alice. "I'm a–I'm a—"

"Well! WHAT are you?" said the Pigeon. "I can see you're trying to invent something!"

"I–I'm a little girl," said Alice.

"A likely story indeed!" said the Pigeon in a tone of the deepest contempt. "I've seen a good many little girls in my time, but never ONE with such a neck as that! No, no! You're a serpent. I suppose you'll be telling me next that you never tasted an egg!"

"I HAVE tasted eggs, certainly," said Alice,

who was a very truthful child; "but little girls eat eggs quite as much as serpents do, you know."

"I don't believe it," said the Pigeon; "but if they do, why then they're a kind of serpent, that's all I can say."

This was such a new idea to Alice that she was quite silent for a minute or two, which gave the Pigeon the opportunity of adding,

"You're looking for eggs, I know THAT well enough; and what does it matter to me whether you're a little girl or a serpent?"

"It matters a lot to ME," said Alice, hastily; "but I'm not looking for eggs, as it happens; and if I was, I shouldn't want YOURS. I don't like them raw."

"Well, be off, then!" said the Pigeon in a sulky tone, as it settled down again into its nest.

Alice crouched down among the trees as well as she could, for her neck kept getting entangled among the branches. Every now and then, she had to stop and untwist it. After a

while she remembered that she still held the pieces of mushroom in her hands. So, she set to work very carefully, nibbling first at one and then at the other, and growing sometimes taller and sometimes shorter. At last she succeeded in bringing herself down to her usual height.

It was so long since she had been anything near the right size, that it felt quite strange at first. But soon she got used to it. Then, she began talking to herself, as usual. 'Come, there's half my plan done now! How puzzling all these changes are! I'm never sure what I'm going to be, from one minute to another! However, I've got back to my right size. Next, I want to get into that beautiful garden—how IS that to be done, I wonder?'

As she said this, suddenly, she found herself in an open place, with a little house in it about four feet high.

'Whoever lives there,' thought Alice, 'would be frightened out of their wits if they see me at

THIS size!'

So, she began nibbling at the right-hand bit again, and did not venture to go near the house till she had brought herself down to nine inches high.

CHAPTER 6

Pig and Pepper

For a minute or two she stood looking at the house, and wondering what to do next, when suddenly a footman in livery came running out of the wood. (Alice considered him to be a footman because he was in livery. Otherwise, judging by his face only, she would have called him a fish.) The footman rapped loudly at the door with his knuckles.

It was opened by another footman in livery, with a round face, and large eyes that resembled a frog. Both footmen had powdered hair that curled all over their heads. Alice felt very curious to know what it was all about, and crept a little way out of the wood to listen.

The Fish-Footman began by producing from under his arm a great letter, nearly as large as himself. This, he handed over to the other, saying, in a solemn tone, "For the Duchess. An invitation from the Queen to play croquet."

The Frog-Footman repeated, in the same solemn tone, only changing the order of the words a little, "From the Queen. An invitation for the Duchess to play croquet."

Then they both bowed low, and their curls got entangled together.

Alice laughed so much at this that she had to run back into the wood for fear of being heard by them.

When she next peeped out, the Fish-

Footman was gone, and the other was sitting on the ground near the door, staring stupidly up into the sky.

Alice went timidly up to the door, and knocked.

"There's no sort of use in knocking," said the Footman, "and that for two reasons. Firstly, because I'm on the same side of the door as you are; secondly, because they're making such a noise inside, that no one could possibly hear you."

Certainly, there was a loud noise coming from within—a constant howling and sneezing, and every now and then a great crash, as if a dish or kettle had been broken to pieces.

"Please, then," said Alice, "how am I to get in?"

"There might be some sense in your knocking," the Footman went on, without attending to her, "if we had the door between us. For instance, if you were INSIDE, you might knock, and I could let you out, you know."

He was looking up into the sky all the time he was speaking, and this Alice thought was very rude.

'But perhaps he can't help it,' she said to herself; 'his eyes are almost at the top of his head. But at any rate he might answer questions.'

"How am I to get in?" she repeated, aloud.

"I shall sit here," the Footman remarked, "till tomorrow—"

At this moment, the door of the house opened, and a large plate came skimming out, straight at the Footman's head. It just brushed past his nose, and broke to pieces against one of the trees behind him. "—or next day, maybe," the Footman continued in the same tone, exactly as if nothing had happened.

"How am I to get in?" asked Alice again, in a louder tone. "ARE you to get in at all?" said the Footman. "That's the first question, you know."

It was, no doubt. Only Alice did not like to be told so. 'It's really dreadful,' she muttered to herself, 'the way all the creatures argue.

It's enough to drive one crazy!'

The Footman seemed to think this as a good opportunity for repeating his remark, with variations. "I shall sit here," he said, "on and off, for days and days."

"But what am I to do?" said Alice.

"Anything you like," said the Footman, and then, he began to whistle.

'Oh, there's no use in talking to him,' said Alice, desperately. 'He's perfectly idiotic!' And she opened the door and went in.

The door led right into a large kitchen, which was full of smoke from one end to the other. The Duchess was sitting on a three-legged stool in the middle, nursing a baby; the cook was leaning over the fire, stirring a large caldron which seemed to be full of soup.

'There's certainly too much pepper in that

soup!' Alice said to herself, sneezing.

There was certainly too much of it in the air. Even the Duchess sneezed occasionally; and as for the baby, it was sneezing and howling alternately without a moment's pause. The only things in the kitchen that did not sneeze were the cook, and a large cat which was sitting on the hearth and grinning from ear to ear.

"Please would you tell me," said Alice, a little timidly, for she was not quite sure whether it was good manners for her to speak first, "why your cat grins like that?"

"It's a Cheshire cat," said the Duchess, "and that's why. Pig!"

She said the last word with such sudden violence that Alice quite jumped. But, she saw in another moment that it was addressed to the baby, and not to her. So, she gathered courage, and went on again:--

"I didn't know that Cheshire cats always grinned; in fact, I didn't know that cats COULD grin."

"They all can," said the Duchess; "and most of them do."

"I don't know of any that do," Alice said very politely, feeling quite pleased to have got into a conversation.

"You don't know much," said the Duchess; "and that's a fact."

Alice did not at all like to be told so.

She thought it would be good to change the subject of the conversation. While she was trying to think of one, the cook took the caldron of soup off the fire, and at once set to work throwing everything within her reach at the Duchess and the baby. The fire irons came first; then followed a shower of saucepans, plates, and dishes.

The Duchess took no notice of them even when they hit her; and the baby was howling so much already, that it was quite impossible to say whether the blows hurt it or not.

"Oh, PLEASE mind what you're doing!" cried Alice, jumping up and down in an agony of terror. 'Oh, there goes his PRECIOUS nose', as an unusually large saucepan flew close by it, and very nearly carried it off.

"If everybody minds their own business," the Duchess said in a hoarse growl, "the world would go round much faster than it does."

"That wouldn't be of any help," said Alice, who felt very glad to get an opportunity of showing off a little of her knowledge. "Just think how much faster the day and night would have to go then! You see, the earth takes twenty-four hours to turn round on its axis—"

"Talking of axes," said the Duchess, "chop off her head!"

Alice glanced rather anxiously at the cook, to see if she meant to take the hint. But the cook was busily stirring the soup, and seemed not to be listening, so Alice went on again, "Twenty-four hours, I THINK; or is it twelve? I—"

"Oh, don't bother ME," cried the Duchess; "I never could abide figures!"

And with that she began nursing her child again, singing a sort of lullaby to it as she did so, and giving it a violent shake at the end of every line.

"Here! You may nurse it a bit, if you like!" the Duchess said to Alice, flinging the baby at her as she spoke. "I must go and get ready to play croquet with the Queen," and she hurried out of the room. The cook threw a frying-pan after her as she went out, but it just missed her.

Alice caught the baby with some difficulty, as it was a queer-shaped little creature, and held out its arms and legs in all directions, 'just like a star-fish,' thought Alice.

The poor little thing was snorting like a steam-engine when she caught it, and kept doubling itself up and straightening itself out again.

As soon as Alice had made out the proper way of nursing it, she carried it out into the open air. 'IF I don't take this child away with me,' thought Alice, 'they're sure to kill it in a day or two. Wouldn't it be murder to leave it behind?'

Alice said the last words out loud, and the little thing grunted in reply.

"Don't grunt," said Alice; "that's not at all a proper way of expressing yourself."

The baby grunted again, and Alice looked very anxiously into its face to see what was wrong with it. There was no doubt that it had a VERY turn-up nose, much more like a snout than a real nose. Also, its eyes were getting extremely small for a baby. Altogether, Alice did not like the look of the thing at all.

'But perhaps it was only sobbing,' she thought, and looked into its eyes again, to see if there were any tears.

No, there were no tears. "If you're going to turn into a pig, my dear," said Alice, seriously, "I'll have nothing more to do with you."

The poor little thing sobbed again (or grunted, it was impossible to say which), and they went on for a while in silence.

Alice was just beginning to think to herself, 'Now, what am I to do with this creature when I take it home?' when it grunted again, so violently, that she looked down into its face in some alarm.

This time there could be NO mistake about it. It was neither more nor less than a pig, and she felt that it would be quite absurd for her to carry it further.

So, she set the little creature down, and felt quite relieved to see it trot away quietly into the wood. 'If it had grown up,' she said to herself, 'it would have made a dreadfully ugly child. But it makes rather a handsome pig, I think.'

And she began thinking over other children she knew, who might do very well as pigs, and was just saying to herself, 'if one only knew the right way to change them—' when, she was a little startled at seeing the Cheshire Cat sitting on a branch of a tree a few yards away.

The Cat only grinned when it saw Alice. It looked good-natured, Alice thought. Still, it had VERY long claws and a great many teeth, so, Alice felt that it ought to be treated with respect.

"Cheshire Puss," she began, rather timidly, as she did not at all know whether it would like the name. However, it only grinned a little wider. 'Come, it is pleased so far,' thought Alice, and she went on.

"Would you please tell me which way I ought to go from here?"

"That depends a lot on where you want to get to," said the Cat.

"I don't care much about that," said Alice.

"Then it doesn't matter which way you go," said the Cat.

"So long as I get SOMEWHERE," Alice added as an explanation.

"Oh, you're sure to do that," said the Cat, "if

you only walk long enough."

Alice felt that this could not be denied, so she tried another question.

"What sort of people live about here?"

"In THAT direction," the Cat said, waving its right paw round, "lives a Hatter, (a 'Hatter' was a person who made hats.); and in THAT direction," waving the other paw, "lives a March Hare. Visit either you like. They're both mad."

"But I don't want to go among mad people," Alice remarked.

"Oh, you can't help that," said the Cat, "we're all mad here. I'm mad. You're mad."

"How do you know I'm mad?" said Alice.

"You must be," said the Cat, "or you would-n't have come here."

Alice didn't think that proved it at all; how-ever, she went on, "And how do you know that you're mad?"

"To begin with," said the Cat, "a dog's not mad. You grant that?"

"I suppose so," said Alice.

"Well, then," the Cat went on, "you see, a dog growls when it's angry, and wags its tail when it's pleased. Now, I growl when I'm pleased, and wag my tail when I'm angry. Therefore, I'm mad."

"I call it purring, not growling," said Alice.

"Call it what you like," said the Cat. "Are you going to play croquet with the Queen today?"

"I should like it very much," said Alice, "but I haven't been invited yet."

"You'll see me there," said the Cat, and vanished.

Alice was not much surprised at this, as, by this time she was quite used to queer things happening around her. While she was looking at the place where it had been, it suddenly appeared again.

"By-the-by, what became of the baby?" said the Cat. "I'd nearly forgotten to ask."

"It turned into a pig," Alice quietly said, just

as if it had come back in a natural way.

"I thought it would," said the Cat, and vanished again.

Alice waited a little, half expecting to see it again, but it did not appear, and after a minute or two she walked on in the direction in which the March Hare was said to live. 'I've seen hatters before,' she said to herself; 'the March Hare will be much the most interesting, and perhaps as this is May it won't be raving mad--at least not so mad as it was in March.'

As she said this, she looked up, and there was the Cat again, sitting on a branch of a tree.

"Did you say pig, or fig?" said the Cat.

"I said pig," replied Alice; "and I wish you wouldn't keep appearing and vanishing so suddenly. You make one quite giddy."

"All right," said the Cat; and this time it vanished quite slowly, beginning with the end of the tail, and ending with the grin, which remained some time after the rest of it had gone.

'Well! I've often seen a cat without a grin,' thought Alice; 'but a grin without a cat! It's the most curious thing I ever saw in my life!'

Alice had not gone much farther before she saw the house of the March Hare. She thought it must be the right house, because the chimneys were shaped like ears and the roof was thatched with fur.

It was so large a house that she did not like to go nearer till she had nibbled some more of the left-hand bit of mushroom, and raised herself to about two feet high.

Even then she walked toward it rather timidly, saying to herself 'Suppose it should be raving mad after all! I almost wish I'd gone to see the Hatter instead!'

CHAPTER 7

A Mad Tea-Party

There was a table set out under a tree in front of the house, and the March Hare and the Hatter were having tea at it.

A Dormouse was sitting between them, fast asleep; the other two were using it as a cushion, resting their elbows on it, and talking over its head.

'Very uncomfortable for the Dormouse,'

thought Alice; 'only, as it's asleep, I suppose it doesn't mind.'

The table was a large one, but the three were all crowded together at one corner of it.

"No room! No room!" they cried out, when they saw Alice approaching.

"There's PLENTY of room!" said Alice, indignantly, and she sat down in a large arm-chair at one end of the table.

"Have some wine," the March Hare said, in an encouraging tone.

Alice looked all round the table, but there was nothing on it but tea.

"I don't see any wine," she remarked.

"There isn't any," said the March Hare.

"Then it wasn't very civil of you to offer it," said Alice, angrily.

"It wasn't very civil of you to sit down without being invited," said the March Hare.

"I didn't know it was YOUR table," said Alice; "it's laid for a great many more than three."

"Your hair wants cutting," said the Hatter. He had been looking at Alice for some time with great curiosity, and this was his first speech.

"You should learn not to make personal remarks," Alice said with some severity; "it's very rude."

The Hatter opened his eyes very wide on hearing this; but all he SAID was, "Why is a raven like a writing-desk?"

'Come, we shall have some fun now!' thought Alice. 'I'm glad they've begun asking riddles.'

"I believe I can guess that," she added aloud.

"Do you mean that you think you can find out the answer to it?" said the March Hare.

"Exactly so," said Alice.

"Then you should say what you mean," the March Hare went on.

"I do," Alice hastily replied; "at least—at least I mean what I say— that's the same thing, you know."

"Not the same thing a bit!" said the Hatter. "You might just as well say that 'I see what I eat' is the same thing as 'I eat what I see'!"

"You might just as well say," added the March Hare, "that 'I like what I get' is the same thing as 'I get what I like'!"

"You might just as well say," added the Dormouse, who seemed to be talking in his sleep, "that 'I breathe when I sleep' is the same thing as 'I sleep when I breathe'!"

"It IS the same thing with you," said the Hatter, and here the conversation dropped, and the party sat silent for a minute.

The Hatter was the first to break the silence. "What day of the month is it?" he said, turning to Alice.

He had taken his watch out of his pocket, and was looking at it uneasily, shaking it every now and then, and holding it to his ear.

Alice considered a little, and then said "The fourth."

"Two days wrong!" the Hatter sighed. "I told you butter wouldn't suit the works!" he added, looking angrily at the March Hare.

"It was the BEST butter," the March Hare meekly replied.

"Yes, but some crumbs must have got in as well," the Hatter grumbled. "You shouldn't have put it in with the bread-knife."

The March Hare took the watch and looked at it gloomily. Then, he dipped it into his cup of tea, and looked at it again. But he could think of nothing better to say than his first remark, "It was the BEST butter, you know."

Alice had been looking over his shoulder with some curiosity. "What a funny watch!" she remarked. "It tells the day of the month, and doesn't tell what o'clock it is!"

"Why should it?" muttered the Hatter. "Does YOUR watch tell you what year it is?"

"Of course not," Alice replied at once. "But that's because it stays the same year for such a long time together."

"Which is just the case with MINE," said the Hatter.

Alice felt dreadfully puzzled. The Hatter's remark seemed to have no sort of meaning in it, and yet it was certainly English. 'I don't quite understand you,' she said, as politely as she could.

"The Dormouse is asleep again," said the Hatter, and he poured a little hot tea upon its nose.

The Dormouse shook its head impatiently, and said, without opening its eyes, "Of course, of course; just what I was going to remark myself."

"Have you guessed the riddle yet?" the Hatter asked, turning to Alice again.

"No, I give up," Alice replied. "What's the answer?"

"I haven't the slightest idea," said the Hatter.

"Nor I," said the March Hare.

Alice sighed, wearily. "I think you might do something better with the time," she said, "rather than waste it in asking riddles that have no answers."

"If you knew Time as well as I do," said the Hatter, "you wouldn't talk about wasting IT. It's HIM."

"I don't know what you mean," said Alice.

"Of course you don't!" the Hatter said, tossing his head contemptuously. "I dare say you never even spoke to Time!"

"Perhaps not," Alice cautiously replied, "but I know I have to beat time when I learn music."

"Ah! That explains it," said the Hatter. "He won't stand beating."

Now, if you only kept on good terms with Time, he'd do almost anything you liked with the clock. For example, suppose it were nine o'clock in the morning – the time to begin lessons, you'd only have to whisper a word to Time, and in a twinkling the clock would move forwards to half-past one: time for dinner!"

('I only wish it was,' the March Hare said to itself in a whisper.)

"That would be grand, certainly," said Alice, thoughtfully. "But then, I shouldn't be hungry for it, you know."

"Not at first, perhaps," said the Hatter. "But you could keep it to halfpast one as long as you liked."

"Is that the way YOU manage?" Alice asked.

The Hatter shook his head mournfully. "Not I!" he replied. "We quarreled last March—just before HE went mad, you know—"(pointing with his tea spoon at the March Hare,) "--it was at the great concert given by the Queen of Hearts, and I had to sing:

'Twinkle, twinkle, little bat!

How I wonder what you're at!'

"You know the song, perhaps?"

"I've heard something like it," said Alice.

"It goes on, you know," the Hatter continued, "in this way:--

'Up above the world you fly,
Like a tea-tray in the sky.
Twinkle, twinkle—' "

Here, the Dormouse shook itself and began singing in its sleep, 'Twinkle, twinkle, twinkle, twinkle—' and went on for so long, that they had to pinch it to make it stop.

"Well, I'd hardly finished the first verse," said the Hatter, "when the Queen jumped up and cried out, 'He's murdering the time! Off with his head!' "

"How dreadfully savage!" exclaimed Alice.

"And ever since that," the Hatter went on in a mournful tone, "he won't do a thing I ask! It's always six o'clock now."

A bright idea came into Alice's head.

"Is that the reason so many tea-things are put out here?" she asked.

"Yes, that's right," said the Hatter with a sigh, "it's always tea-time, and we've no time to wash the things between whiles."

"Then you keep moving round, I suppose?" said Alice. "Exactly so," said the Hatter, "as the things get used up."

"But what happens when you come to the beginning again?" Alice asked.

"Suppose we change the subject," the March Hare interrupted, yawning. "I'm getting tired of this. I vote the young lady tells us a story."

"I'm afraid I don't know one," said Alice, rather alarmed at the proposal.

"Then the Dormouse shall!" they both cried. "Wake up, Dormouse!"

And they pinched it on both sides at once.

The Dormouse slowly opened his eyes. "I wasn't asleep," he said in a hoarse, feeble voice, "I heard every word all of you were saying."

"Tell us a story!" said the March Hare.

"Yes, please do!" pleaded Alice.

"And be quick about it," added the Hatter,

"or you'll be asleep again before it's done."

"Once upon a time there were three little sisters," the Dormouse began in a great hurry; "and their names were Elsie, Lacie, and Tillie; and they lived at the bottom of a well—"

"What did they live on?" asked Alice, who always took a great interest in questions of eating and drinking.

"They lived on treacle," said the Dormouse, after thinking a minute or two.

"They couldn't have done that, you know," Alice gently remarked; "they'd have been ill."

"So they were," said the Dormouse, "VERY ill."

Alice tried to imagine what such an extraordinary way of living would be like. But, it puzzled her too much, so she went on, "But why did they live at the bottom of a well?"

"Take some more tea," the March Hare said to Alice, very earnestly.

"I've had nothing yet," Alice replied in an

offended tone, "so I can't take more."

"You mean you can't take LESS," said the Hatter, "it's very easy to take MORE than nothing."

"Nobody asked YOUR opinion," said Alice.

"Who's making personal remarks now?" the Hatter asked, triumphantly.

Alice did not quite know what to say to this. So, she helped herself to some tea and bread-and-butter. Then, she turned to the Dormouse, and repeated her question, "Why did they live at the bottom of a well?"

The Dormouse again took a minute or two to think about it, and then said, "It was a treacle-well."

"There's no such thing!" Alice was beginning very angrily, but the Hatter and the March Hare went "Sh! sh!" and the Dormouse sulkily remarked, "If you can't be civil, you'd better finish the story for yourself."

"No, please go on!" Alice said very humbly;

"I won't interrupt again. I dare say there may be ONE."

"One, indeed!" said the Dormouse, indignantly. However, he consented to go on. "And so these three little sisters— they were learning to draw, you know—"

"What did they draw?" said Alice, quite forgetting her promise.

"Treacle," said the Dormouse, without considering at all this time.

"I want a clean cup," interrupted the Hatter; "let's all move one place on."

He moved on as he spoke, and the Dormouse followed him. The March Hare moved into the Dormouse's place, and Alice rather unwillingly took the place of the March Hare. The Hatter was the only one who got any advantage from the change. But, Alice was worse off than before, as the March Hare had just upset the milk-jug into his plate.

Alice did not wish to offend the Dormouse

again, so she began very cautiously, "But I don't understand. Where did they draw the treacle from?"

"You can draw water out of a water-well," said the Hatter; "so I should think you could draw treacle out of a treacle-well-eh, stupid?"

"But they were IN the well," Alice said to the Dormouse, not choosing to notice this last remark.

"Of course they were," said the Dormouse; "-well in."

This answer confused poor Alice so much, that she let the Dormouse go on for some time without interrupting it.

"They were learning to draw," the Dormouse went on, yawning and rubbing its eyes, for it was getting very sleepy; "and they drew all manner of things-everything that begins with an M-"

"Why with an M?" said Alice.

"Why not?" said the March Hare.

Alice was silent.

The Dormouse had closed its eyes by this time, and was going off into a doze. But, on being pinched by the Hatter, it woke up again with a little shriek, and went on "—that begins with an M, such as mouse-traps, and the moon, and memory, and muchness— you know you say things are 'much of a muchness'—did you ever see such a thing as a drawing of a muchness?"

"Really, now you ask me," said Alice, very much confused, "I don't think—"

"Then you shouldn't talk," said the Hatter. This piece of rudeness was more than Alice could bear. She got up in great disgust, and walked off. The Dormouse fell asleep instantly, and neither of the others took the least notice of her going, though Alice looked back once or twice, half hoping that they would call after her. The last time she saw them, they were trying to put the Dormouse into the teapot.

'At any rate I'll never go THERE again!' said

Alice, as she picked her way through the wood. 'It's the stupidest tea-party I ever attended!'

Just as she said this, she noticed that one of the trees had a door leading right into it. 'That's very curious!' she thought. 'But everything's curious today. I think I may as well go in at once.' And in she went.

Once more Alice found herself in the long hall and close to the little glass table.

'Now, I'll manage better this time,' she said to herself, and began by taking the little golden key, and unlocking the door that led into the garden. She began nibbling at the mushroom (she had kept a piece of it in her pocket) till she was about a foot high. Then, she walked down the little passage and THEN found herself, at last, in the beautiful garden, among the bright flower-beds and the cool fountains.

CHAPTER 8

The Queen's Croquet-Ground

A large rose-tree stood near the entrance of the garden. The roses growing on it were white, but there were three gardeners who were busy painting them red.

Alice thought this to be a very curious thing, and she went nearer to watch them. Just as she went near them, she heard one of them say, "Look out now, Five! Don't go splashing paint over me like that!"

"I couldn't help it," replied Five, in a sulky tone; "Seven shoved my elbow!"

Seven looked up immediately and said, "That's right, Five! Always lay the blame on others!"

"YOU'D better not talk!" said Five. "I heard the Queen say only yesterday that you deserved to be beheaded!"

"What for?" asked the one who had spoken first. "That's none of YOUR business, Two!" said Seven. "Yes, it IS his business!" said Five, "and I'll tell him—it was for bringing the cook tulip-roots instead of onions."

Seven flung down his brush, and had just begun, "Well, of all the unjust things…" when his eye chanced to fall upon Alice, as she stood watching them, and he stopped himself suddenly. The others looked round also, and all of them bowed low.

"Would you tell me," said Alice, a little timidly, "why you are painting those roses?"

Five and Seven said nothing, but looked at Two. Two began in a low voice, "Why the fact is, you see, Miss, this—here ought to have been a RED rose-tree, and we put a white one in by mistake. Now, if the Queen was to find it out, we should all have our heads cut off, you know. So you see, Miss, we're doing our best, before she comes, to—"

At this moment Five, who had been anxiously looking across the garden, called out, "The Queen! The Queen!" and the three gardeners instantly threw themselves flat upon their faces.

There was a sound of many footsteps, and Alice looked round, eager to see the Queen.

First, ten soldiers marched in carrying clubs. They were all shaped like the three gardeners, oblong and flat, with their hands and feet at the corners. Next, came in the ten courtiers. They were wearing diamonds all over, and walked two and two, as the soldiers did.

After them came the royal children; there were ten of them, and the little dears came jumping merrily. They were all ornamented with hearts. Next came the guests, mostly Kings and Queens, and among them Alice recognized the White Rabbit. It was talking in a hurried nervous manner, smiling at everything that was said, and went by without noticing Alice.

The Knave of Hearts came next, carrying the King's crown on a crimson velvet cushion. Then last of all, came THE KING AND QUEEN OF HEARTS.

Alice was doubtful whether she should lie down on her face like the three gardeners or not. But, she could not remember having heard of such a rule at processions; 'and besides, what would be the use of a procession,' thought she, 'if people had all to lie down upon their faces, so that they couldn't see it?' So, she stood still where she was, and waited.

When the procession came opposite to

Alice, they all stopped and looked at her. "Who is this?" The Queen questioned the Knave of Hearts, who only bowed and smiled in reply.

"Idiot!" said the Queen, tossing her head impatiently; and, turning to Alice, she went on, "what's your name, child?"

"My name is Alice, your Majesty," said Alice, very politely. But, she added, to herself, 'Why, they're only a pack of cards, after all. I have no reason be afraid of them!'

"And who are THESE?" asked the Queen, pointing to the three gardeners who were lying round the rose tree.

"How should I know?" replied Alice, surprised at her own courage.

"It's no business of MINE."

The Queen turned crimson with fury, and, after glaring at Alice for a moment like a wild beast, screamed, "Off with her head! Off—"

"Nonsense!" said Alice, very loudly, and the Queen was silent.

The King laid his hand upon her arm, and timidly said, "Consider, my dear, she is only a child!"

The Queen turned angrily away from him, and said to the Knave "Turn them over!"

The Knave did so, very carefully, with one foot. "Get up!" said the Queen, in a shrill, loud voice, and the three gardeners instantly jumped up. As soon as they were on their feet, they began bowing to the King, the Queen, the royal children, and everybody else.

"Stop that!" screamed the Queen. "You make me giddy."

And then, turning to the rose-tree, she went on, "What HAVE you been doing here?"

"May it please your Majesty," said Two, in a very humble tone, going down on one knee as he spoke, "we were trying—"

"I see!" said the Queen, who had meanwhile been examining the roses.

"Off with their heads!"

And the procession moved on, three of the soldiers remaining behind to execute the unfortunate gardeners, who ran to Alice for protection.

"You shall not be beheaded!" said Alice, and she put them into a large flower-pot that stood near.

The three soldiers wandered about for a minute or two, looking for them, and then quietly marched off after the others.

"Are their heads off?" shouted the Queen.

"Their heads are gone, if it pleases your Majesty!" the soldiers replied.

"That's right!" shouted the Queen. "Can you play croquet?" The soldiers were silent, and looked at Alice, as the question was evidently meant for her.

"Yes!" shouted Alice.

"Come on, then!" roared the Queen, and Alice joined the procession, wondering curiously about what would happen next.

"It's...it's a very fine day!" said a timid voice at her side. She was walking by the White Rabbit, who was peeping anxiously into her face.

"Very," said Alice, "where's the Duchess?"

"Hush! Hush!" said the Rabbit in a low, hurried tone. He looked anxiously over his shoulder as he spoke, and then raised himself upon tiptoe, put his mouth close to her ear, and whispered, "She has been sentenced to be executed."

"What for?" asked Alice. "Did you say 'What a pity!'?" the Rabbit asked.

"No, I didn't," said Alice, "I don't think it's at all a pity." "I asked, 'What for?'"

"She boxed the Queen's ears..." the Rabbit began. Alice gave a little scream of laughter. "Oh, hush!" the Rabbit whispered in a frightened tone. "The Queen will hear you! You see, she came rather late, and the Queen said—"

'Get to your places!' shouted the Queen in

a voice of thunder, and people began running about in all directions, tumbling up against each other. However, they got settled down in a minute or two, and the game began.

Alice thought she had never seen such a curious croquet-ground in her life. It was all ridges and furrows; the balls were live hedge-hogs, the mallets – live flamingoes, and the soldiers had to double themselves up and to stand on their hands and feet, to make the arches.

The chief difficulty Alice found at first was in managing her flamingo. The players all played at once without waiting for turns, quarreling all the while, and fighting for the hedgehogs. In a very short time the Queen was furious, and went stamping about, and shouting 'Off with his head!' or 'Off with her head!' about once in a minute.

Alice soon concluded that it was a very difficult game indeed and she began to feel very uneasy. She had not as yet had any dispute with the Queen, but she knew that it might happen any minute, 'and then,' thought she, 'what would become of me? They're dreadfully fond of beheading people here. It's a wonder that people are alive over here!'

Alice was looking about for some way of escape, and wondering whether she could get away without being seen. All of a sudden, she noticed a curious appearance in the air. It puzzled her very much at first, but, after watching it a minute or two, she could make out that it was a grin. 'It's the Cheshire Cat,' Alice said to herself, 'now I shall have somebody to talk to.'

"How are you getting on?" said the Cat, as soon as there was mouth enough for it to speak with.

Alice waited till the eyes appeared, and then nodded. 'It's no use speaking to it,' she thought, 'till its ears have come, or at least one of them.' In another minute the whole head appeared, and then Alice put down her flamingo, and began an account of the game. She felt glad that she had someone to listen to her.

"I don't think they play fairly at all," Alice began, in a rather complaining tone, "and they all quarrel so dreadfully that one can't hear one's own voice! They don't seem to have any rules; and if there are any, nobody follows them!"

"How do you like the Queen?" said the Cat in a low voice. "Not at all," replied Alice, "she's so extremely—"

Just then, Alice noticed that the Queen was close behind her, listening.

So, she went on, "…likely to win, that it's hardly worth while finishing the game."

The Queen smiled and passed on.

"Who ARE you talking to?" said the King, going up to Alice, and looking at the Cat's head with great curiosity.

"It's a friend of mine—a Cheshire Cat," said Alice, "allow me to introduce it."

"I don't like the look of it at all," said the

King, "however, it may kiss my hand if it likes."

"I'd rather not," the Cat remarked.

"Don't be impolite," said the King, "and don't look at me like that!"

The king got behind Alice as he spoke.

"A cat may look at a king," said Alice. "I've read that in some book, but I don't remember where."

"Well, it must be removed," said the King, very sternly. Then he called the Queen, who was passing at the moment, "My dear! I wish you would have this cat removed!"

The Queen had only one way of dealing with all difficulties, great or small– "Off with his head!" she said, without even looking round.

"I'll fetch the executioner myself," said the King, eagerly, and he hurried off.

Alice thought she might as well go back, and see how the game was going on, as she heard the Queen's voice in the distance, screaming with passion. She had already heard her sentencing three of the players to be executed for having missed their turns. Alice did not like the way the things were going on. The game was so chaotic that she never knew whether it was her turn or not. So, she went about in search of her hedgehog.

The hedgehog was engaged in a fight with another hedgehog, which seemed to Alice an excellent opportunity for croqueting one of them with the other. The only difficulty was that her flamingo had gone across to the other side of the garden, where Alice could see it trying in a helpless sort of way to fly up into a tree.

By the time she had caught the flamingo and brought it back, the fight was over, and both the hedgehogs were out of sight. 'But it doesn't matter much,' thought Alice, 'as all the arches are gone from the side of the ground.'

So, she tucked it away under her arm, so that it might not escape again, and went back for a little more conversation with her friend.

When Alice got back to the Cheshire Cat, she was surprised to find quite a large crowd collected round it. There was a dispute going on between the executioner, the King, and the Queen, who were all talking at once, while all the rest were quite silent, and looked very uncomfortable.

The moment Alice appeared all the three requested her to settle the question. They repeated their arguments to her, though, as they all spoke at once, she found it very hard to make out exactly what they were saying.

The executioner's argument was that you couldn't cut off a head unless there was a body to cut it off from. He said that he had never done such a thing before, and he wasn't going to begin at HIS time of life.

The King's argument was that anything that had a head could be beheaded.

The Queen's argument was that if something wasn't done about it, she would have everybody executed very soon. Alice could think of nothing else to say, but, "It belongs to the Duchess. You'd better ask HER about it."

"She's in prison," the Queen said to the executioner; "Bring her over here." And the executioner went off like an arrow.

The Cat's head began fading away the moment he was gone, and, by the time he had come back with the Duchess, it had entirely disappeared.

So, the King and the executioner ran wildly up and down looking for it, while the rest of the party went back to the game.

CHAPTER 9

The Mock Turtle's Story

O Dear! You can't imagine how glad I am to see you again!' said the Duchess, as she tucked her arm affectionately into Alice's, and they walked off together.

Alice was very glad to find her in such a pleasant temper. She thought to herself that perhaps it was only the pepper that had made the Duchess so savage when they had met in the kitchen.

'When I'M a Duchess,' Alice said to herself, 'I won't have any pepper in my kitchen AT ALL. Soup does very well without it. Maybe it's always pepper that makes people hot-tempered,' she went on, 'and vinegar that makes them sour. And maybe, Camomile makes people bitter. Also, it may be that barley-sugar and such things make children sweet-tempered. I only wish people knew that. Then they wouldn't be so stingy about it, you know—'

Alice had quite forgotten the Duchess by this time. She was startled when she heard the Duchess' voice close to her ear, "You're thinking about something, my dear, and that makes you forget to talk. I can't tell you just now what the moral of that is, but I shall remember it in a bit."

"Perhaps it doesn't have a moral," Alice remarked.

"Tut, tut, child!" said the Duchess. "Everything's got a moral, if only you can find it."

And as she spoke, she squeezed herself close to Alice.

Alice didn't like this: firstly, because the Duchess was VERY ugly; and secondly, because she was exactly the right height to rest her chin upon Alice's shoulder. Moreover, hers was an uncomfortably sharp chin.

However, Alice did not like to be rude, so, she bore it as well as she could.

"The game's going on rather better now," she said, by way of keeping up the conversation a little.

"So it is," agreed the Duchess, "and the moral of that is—Oh, it is love, it is love, that makes the world go round!"

"Somebody said," Alice whispered, "that it's done by everybody minding their own business!"

"Ah, well! It means almost the same thing," said the Duchess, digging her sharp little chin into Alice's shoulder as she added, "and the

moral of THAT is— 'Take care of the sense, and the sounds will take care of themselves.' "

'How fond she is of finding morals in things!' Alice thought to herself.

"I dare say you're wondering why I don't put my arm round your waist," the Duchess said after a pause, "the reason is that I'm doubtful about the temper of your flamingo. Shall I try this experiment?"

"HE might bite," Alice replied, not feeling at all anxious to have the experiment tried.

"Very true," said the Duchess, "flamingoes and mustard both bite. And the moral of that is—'Birds of a feather flock together.' "

"Only mustard isn't a bird," Alice remarked.

"Right, as usual," said the Duchess, "what a good way you have of putting things!"

"It's a mineral, I THINK," said Alice.

"Of course it is," said the Duchess, who seemed ready to agree to everything that Alice said; "there's a large mustard-mine nearby.

And the moral of that is—'The more there is of mine, the less there is of yours.' "

"Oh, I know!" exclaimed Alice, who had not attended to this last remark, "it's a vegetable. It doesn't look like one, but it is."

"I quite agree with you," said the Duchess; "and the moral of that is—'Be what you would seem to be'—or if you'd like to put it more simply—'Never imagine yourself not to be otherwise than what it might appear to others that what you were or might have been was not otherwise than what you had been would have appeared to them to be otherwise.' "

"I think I should understand that better if I had it written down, and I could read it," Alice said, very politely. "But, I can't quite follow it as you say it."

"That's nothing to what I could say if I chose," the Duchess replied, in quite a pleased tone.

"Please don't trouble yourself to say it any

longer than that," said Alice.

"Oh, don't talk about trouble!" said the Duchess. "I'm now making you a present of everything I've said till now."

'A cheap sort of present!' thought Alice. 'I'm glad they don't give birthday presents like that!'

But she decided not to say this aloud.

"Thinking again?" the Duchess asked, with another dig of her sharp little chin.

"I've a right to think," said Alice, sharply, for she was beginning to feel a little worried.

"Just about as much right," said the Duchess, "as pigs have to fly, and the m—" But here, to Alice's great surprise, the Duchess's voice died away, even in the middle of her favorite word 'moral,' while the arm that was linked into Alice's, began to tremble.

Alice looked up, and there stood the Queen in front of them, with her arms folded. She was frowning like a thunderstorm.

"A fine day, your Majesty!" the Duchess

began in a low, weak voice. "Now, I give you fair warning," shouted the Queen, stamping on the ground as she spoke; "either you or your head must be off, and that in about half no time! Take your choice!"

The Duchess took her choice, and was gone in a moment. "Let's go on with the game," the Queen said to Alice.

Alice slowly followed her back to the croquet-ground. The other guests had taken advantage of the Queen's absence, and were resting in the shade. However, the moment they saw her, they hurried back to the game, the Queen merely remarking that a moment's delay would cost them their lives.

All the time they were playing the Queen never left off quarreling with the other players, and shouting, 'Off with his head!' or 'Off with her head!'

Those whom she sentenced were taken into custody by the soldiers, who of course had to leave off being arches to do this, so that by the end of half an hour or so there were no arches left, and all the players, except the King, the Queen, and Alice, were in custody and under sentence of execution.

Then the Queen left off, quite out of breath, and asked Alice, "Have you seen the Mock Turtle yet?"

"No," said Alice. "I don't even know what a Mock Turtle is."

"It's the thing Mock Turtle Soup is made from," said the Queen.

"I never saw one, or heard of one," said Alice.

"Come on, then," said the Queen, "and he shall tell you his history."

As they walked off together, Alice heard the King say in a low voice to the company in general, "You are all pardoned."

'Come, THAT'S a good thing,' thought Alice, for she had felt quite unhappy at the number of executions the Queen had ordered.

Very soon, they came upon a Gryphon, lying fast asleep in the sun.

Now, the Gryphon was a beast having the head and wings and front claws of an eagle, along with the body, rear paws and tail of a lion.

"Up, lazy thing!" said the Queen, "and take this young lady to see the Mock Turtle, and to hear his history. I must go back and see after some executions I have ordered"; and she walked off, leaving Alice alone with the Gryphon. Alice did not quite like the look of the creature, but on the whole she thought it would be quite safe to stay with it than to go after the savage Queen. So, she waited. The Gryphon sat up and rubbed its eyes. Then, it watched the Queen till she was out of sight. And when she could no longer be seen, the Gryphon chuck-led.

"What fun!" said the Gryphon, half to itself, half to Alice.

"What IS the fun?" said Alice.

"Why, SHE," said the Gryphon. "It's all her fancy. They never execute anybody, you know. Come on!"

'Everybody says "come on!" here,' thought Alice, as she went slowly after it. 'I was never ordered about like this, in all my life, never!'

They had not gone far, before they saw the Mock Turtle in the distance, sitting sad and lonely on a little ledge of rock. As they came nearer, Alice could hear him sighing as if his heart would break.

"What is his sorrow?" she asked the Gryphon, and the Gryphon answered, "It's all his fancy. He hasn't got any sorrow, you know. Come on!"

So they went up to the Mock Turtle, who looked at them with large eyes full of tears.

"This young lady," said the Gryphon, "wants to know your history."

"I'll tell her," said the Mock Turtle in a deep,

hollow tone, "sit down, both of you, and don't speak a word till I've finished."

So they sat down, and nobody spoke for a few minutes.

Alice thought to herself, "I don't see how he can EVEN finish, if he doesn't begin."

However, she waited patiently.

"Once," said the Mock Turtle at last, with a deep sigh, "I was a real Turtle."

These words were followed by a very long silence, broken only by an occasional exclamation of 'Hjckrrh!' from the Gryphon, and the constant heavy sobbing of the Mock Turtle.

Alice was very nearly getting up and saying, "Thank you, sir, for your interesting story," but she could not help thinking there MUST be more to come, so she sat still and said nothing.

"When we were little," the Mock Turtle went on at last, more calmly, "we went to school in the sea. The master was an old Turtle. We used to call him Tortoise."

"We had the best of educations. In fact, we went to school every day," the Mock Turtle continued.

"I'VE been to a day-school, too," interrupted Alice; "you needn't be so proud like that."

"With extras?" asked the Mock Turtle, a little anxiously.

"Yes," said Alice, "we learned French and music."

"And washing?" asked the Mock Turtle.

"Certainly not!" said Alice, indignantly.

"Ah! Then yours wasn't a really good school," said the Mock Turtle, in a tone of great relief. "Now at OURS they had at the end of the bill, 'French, music, AND WASHING—extra.'"

"You couldn't have wanted it much," said Alice; "living at the bottom of the sea."

"I couldn't afford to learn it," said the Mock Turtle with a sigh. "I only took the regular course."

"What was that?" inquired Alice.

"Reeling and Writhing, of course, to begin with," the Mock Turtle replied; "and then the different branches of Arithmetic— Ambition, Distraction, Uglification, and Derision."

"I never heard of Uglification," Alice said. "What is it?" The Gryphon lifted up both its paws in surprise. "What! Never heard of uglifying!" it exclaimed. "You know what to beautify is, I suppose?"

"Yes," said Alice, doubtfully, "it means—to—make—anything— prettier."

"Well, then," the Gryphon went on, "if you don't know what to uglify is, you ARE a simpleton."

Alice did not feel encouraged to ask any more questions about it, so she turned to the Mock Turtle, and said, "What else had you to learn?"

"Well, there was Mystery," the Mock Turtle replied, counting off the subjects on his flappers,

"Mystery, ancient and modern, with Seaography. Then, there was Drawling. The Drawling-master was an old conger-eel that used to come once a week. HE taught us Drawling, Stretching, and Fainting in Coils."

"That's enough about lessons," the Gryphon interrupted in a very decided tone, "tell her something about the games now."

CHAPTER 10.

The Lobster Quadrille

The Mock Turtle sighed deeply, and drew the back of one flapper across his eyes. He looked at Alice, and tried to speak, but for a minute or two sobs choked his voice. "It is just as if he had a bone in his throat," said the Gryphon. And it set to work shaking the Mock Turtle and punching him in the back.

At last the Mock Turtle recovered his voice,

and, he went on again:--

"You may not have lived much under the sea and perhaps you were never even introduced to a lobster--" (Alice began to say 'I once tasted-' but checked herself hastily, and said, "No, never.")

"--so you would have no idea what a delightful thing a Lobster Quadrille is!"

"No, indeed," said Alice. "But, I would like to know what sort of a dance is it?"

"Why," said the Gryphon, "you first form into a line along the seashore--"

"Two lines!" cried the Mock Turtle. "Seals, turtles, salmon, and so on; then, when you've cleared all the jelly-fish out of the way you advance twice--"

"Each with a lobster as a partner!" interrupted the Gryphon.

"Of course," the Mock Turtle said, "advance twice, set to partners--"

"--change lobsters, and retire in same order,"

continued the Gryphon. "Then, you know," the Mock Turtle went on, "you throw the—"

"The lobsters!" shouted the Gryphon.

"—as far out to sea as you can—"

"Swim after them!" screamed the Gryphon.

"Back to land again, and that's the first figure of the dance," said the Mock Turtle, suddenly dropping his voice. Meanwhile, the two creatures, who had been jumping about like mad things all this time, sat down again very sadly and quietly, and looked at Alice.

"It must be a very pretty dance," said Alice, timidly. "Would you like to see a little of it?" said the Mock Turtle. "Come, let's try the first figure!" said the Mock Turtle to the Gryphon. "We can do without lobsters, you know. Who shall sing?"

"Oh, YOU sing," said the Gryphon. "I've forgotten the words."

And so, they began solemnly dancing round and round Alice. The Mock Turtle sang this, very slowly and sadly:--

'Will you walk a little faster?'
Said a whiting to a snail.
'There's a porpoise close behind us
And he's treading on my tail.

See how eagerly the lobsters
And the turtles all advance!
They are waiting on the shingle
Will you come and join the dance?

Will you, won't you, will you, won't you
Will you join the dance?

You can really have no notion
How delightful it will be
When they take us up and throw us
With the lobsters, out to sea!'

But the snail replied, 'Too far, too far!'
And gave a look askance,
Said he thanked the whiting kindly

But he would not join the dance.

Would not, could not
Would not, could not
Would not join the dance.

Would not, could not
Would not, could not
Would not join the dance.

'What matters it how far we go?'
His scaly friend replied.
'There is another shore, you know
Upon the other side.
The further off from England,
The nearer is to France
Then turn not pale, beloved snail,
But come and join the dance.

Will you, won't you,
Will you, won't you,

Will you join the dance?

Will you, won't you,
Will you, won't you,
Won't you join the dance?'

"Thank you, it's a very interesting dance to watch," said Alice, "I never knew so much about a whiting before."

"I can tell you more than that, if you like," said the Gryphon. "Do you know why it's called a whiting?"

"I never thought about it," said Alice. "Why?"

"IT DOES THE BOOTS AND SHOES," the Gryphon replied very solemnly.

Alice was thoroughly puzzled. 'Does the boots and shoes!' she repeated in a wondering tone.

"Why, what are YOUR shoes done with?" said the Gryphon. "I mean, what makes them so shiny?"

Alice looked down at them, and considered a little before she gave her answer. "They're done with blacking, I believe."

"Boots and shoes under the sea," the Gryphon explained in a deep voice, "are done with a whiting."

"And what are they made of?" Alice asked, curiously.

"Soles and eels, of course," the Gryphon replied rather impatiently, "any shrimp could have told you that."

"If I'd been the whiting," said Alice, whose thoughts were still running on the song, "I'd have said to the porpoise, 'Keep back, please. We don't want YOU with us!'"

"They were obliged to have him with them," the Mock Turtle said, "no wise fish would go anywhere without a porpoise."

"Wouldn't it really?" said Alice, surprised.

"Of course not," said the Mock Turtle, "why, if a fish came to ME, and told me he was going on a journey, I should say 'With what por-poise?'"

"Don't you mean 'purpose'?" said Alice.

"I mean what I say," the Mock Turtle replied in an offended tone.

"Come now, let's hear some of YOUR adventures," the Gryphon said to Alice.

"I could tell you my adventures beginning from this morning," said Alice, a little timidly, "but it's no use going back to yesterday, because I was a different person then."

"Explain all that," said the Mock Turtle.

"No, no! The adventures first," said the Gryphon in an impatient tone, "explanations take such a dreadful time."

So, Alice began telling them about her adventures from the time when she first saw the White Rabbit. She felt a little nervous about it.

This was because the two creatures moved closer to her, one on each side, and opened their eyes and mouths VERY wide. However, she gained courage as she went on.

After a long while the Gryphon said to Alice, "I think you'd better stop now."

Alice was only too glad to do so.

"Shall we try another figure of the Lobster Quadrille?" the Gryphon went on, "Or would you like the Mock Turtle to sing you a song?"

"Oh, a song, please, if the Mock Turtle would be so kind," Alice replied, so eagerly that the Gryphon said, in a rather offended tone,

"Hm! No accounting for tastes! Sing her 'Turtle Soup,' will you, old fellow?"

The Mock Turtle sighed deeply, and began this song, sometimes choking and bursting into sobs as it sang:

"Beautiful Soup, so rich and green,
Waiting in a hot tureen!
Who for such dainties would not stoop?
Soup of the evening, beautiful Soup!
Soup of the evening, beautiful Soup!

Beau–ootiful Soo–oop!
Beau–ootiful Soo–oop!
Soo–oop of the e–e–evening,
Beautiful, beautiful Soup!
Beautiful Soup! Who cares for fish,
Game, or any other dish?
Who would not give all else for
two pennyworth only of beautiful Soup?
Pennyworth only of beautiful Soup?
Beau–ootiful Soo–oop!
Beau–ootiful Soo–oop!
Soo–oop of the e–e–evening,
Beautiful, beauti–FUL SOUP!''

''Chorus again!'' cried the Gryphon, and the Mock Turtle had just begun to repeat it, when a cry of 'The trial's beginning!' was heard in the distance.

''Come on!'' cried the Gryphon, and, taking Alice by the hand, it hurried off, without waiting for the song to end.

''What trial is it?'' Alice panted, as she ran;

but the Gryphon only answered, "Come on!" and ran even faster, while more and more faintly came, carried on the breeze that followed them, the melancholy words:–

'Soo–oop of the e–e–evening,
Beautiful, beautiful Soup!'

CHAPTER 11

Who Stole the Tarts?

The King and Queen of Hearts were seated on their throne when they arrived. A huge crowd was assembled about them—all sorts of little birds and beasts, as well as the whole pack of cards. The Knave was standing before them, in chains, with a soldier on each side to guard him. Near the King was the White Rabbit, with a trumpet in one hand, and a scroll of parchment in the other.

In the centre of the court was a table, with a large dish of tarts upon it. They looked so good, that it made Alice quite hungry to look at them. 'I wish they'd quickly get over with the trial,' she thought, 'and hand round the refreshments!'

But there seemed to be no chance of this. So, she began looking at everything around her.

Alice had never been in a court of justice before, but she had read about them in books. She was quite pleased to find that she knew the name of nearly everything there. 'That's the judge,' she said to herself, 'because of his great wig.'

The judge was actually the King; and as he wore his crown over the wig, he did not look at all comfortable.

'And that's the jury-box,' thought Alice, 'and those twelve creatures,' (she was obliged to say 'creatures,' you see, because some of them were animals, and some were birds,) 'I suppose they are the jurors.'

The twelve jurors were all writing very busily on slates.

"What are they doing?" Alice whispered to the Gryphon. "They can't have anything to put down yet, before the trial's begun."

"They're putting down their names," the Gryphon whispered in reply, "for fear they should forget them before the end of the trial."

"Stupid things!" Alice began in a loud, indignant voice. However, she had to stop hastily, for the White Rabbit cried out, 'Silence in the court!' and the King put on his spectacles and looked anxiously round, to make out who was talking.

Alice could see, as well as if she were looking over their shoulders that all the jurors were writing down, 'stupid things!' on their slates.

She could even make out that one of them didn't know how to spell 'stupid', and that he

had to ask his neighbor to tell him.

'Their slates will be in a nice muddle before the trial is over!' thought Alice.

"Herald, read the accusation!" ordered the King.

On this, the White Rabbit blew three blasts on the trumpet, and then unrolled the parchment scroll, and read as follows:--

'The Queen of Hearts,
she made some tarts,
All on a summer day:
The Knave of Hearts,
he stole those tarts,
And took them quite away!'

"Consider your verdict," the King said to the jury. "Not yet, not yet!" the Rabbit hastily interrupted. "There's a great deal to come before that!"

"Call the first witness," said the King; and the White Rabbit blew three blasts on the trumpet, and called out, 'First witness!'

The first witness was the Hatter. He came in with a teacup in one hand and a piece of bread-and-butter in the other. "I beg pardon, your Majesty," he began, "for bringing these in. But, I hadn't quite finished my tea when I was sent for."

"You ought to have finished," said the King. "When did you begin?"

The Hatter looked at the March Hare, who had followed him into the court, arm-in-arm with the Dormouse. "Fourteenth of March, I think it was," he said.

"Fifteenth," said the March Hare.

"Sixteenth," added the Dormouse.

"Write that down," the King said to the jury, and the jury eagerly wrote down all three dates on their slates. Then, they added up the dates, and reduced the answer to shillings and pence.

Here, the Queen put on her spectacles, and began staring at the Hatter, who turned pale and fidgeted.

"Give your evidence," said the King; "and don't be nervous, or I'll have you executed on the spot."

This did not seem to encourage the witness at all. He kept shifting from one foot to the other, looking uneasily at the Queen. In his confusion he bit a large piece out of his teacup instead of the bread-and-butter.

Just at this moment Alice felt a very curious sensation, which puzzled her a good deal until she made out what it was. She was beginning to grow larger again, and she thought at first that she would get up and leave the court; but, on second thoughts she decided to remain where she was.

All this time the Queen had never left off staring at the Hatter, and, just as the Dormouse crossed the court, she said to one of the officers of the court, "Bring me the list of the singers in the last concert!"

On hearing this, the wretched Hatter began

to tremble so much that he shook both his shoes off.

"Give your evidence," the King repeated angrily, "or I'll have you executed, whether you're nervous or not."

"I'm a poor man, your Majesty," the Hatter began, in a trembling voice, "—and I hadn't begun my tea—not above a week or so. And what with the bread-and-butter getting so thin, and the twinkling of the tea—"

"The twinkling of the what?" asked the King.

"It began with the tea," the Hatter replied.

"Of course twinkling begins with a T!" said the King sharply. "Do you take me for a fool? Go on!"

"I'm a poor man," the Hatter went on, "and most things twinkled after that. Only the March Hare said—"

"I didn't!" said the Hatter.

"I deny it!" said the King, "leave out that part."

"Well, at any rate, the Dormouse said…" the Hatter went on, looking anxiously round to see if the Dormouse would deny it too. But the Dormouse denied nothing, being fast asleep.

"After that," continued the Hatter, "I cut some more bread-and-butter—"

"But what did the Dormouse say?" one of the jury asked. "That I can't remember," said the Hatter. "You MUST remember," the King remarked, "or I'll have you executed."

The miserable Hatter dropped his teacup and bread-and-butter, and went down on one knee. "I'm a poor man, your Majesty," he began.

"You're a very poor speaker," said the King. "You may go." On hearing this, the Hatter hurriedly left the court.

"—and just take his head off outside," the Queen added to one of the officers. But the Hatter was out of sight before the officer could get to the door.

"Call the next witness!" said the King.

The next witness was the Duchess's cook. She carried the pepper-box in her hand. The people near the door began sneezing all at once.

"Give your evidence," said the King.

"Shall not," said the cook.

The King looked anxiously at the White Rabbit, who said in a low voice, "Your Majesty must cross-examine THIS witness."

"Well, if I must, I must," the King said, with a melancholy air. Then, after staring blankly at the cook for a while, he asked, "What are tarts made of?"

"Pepper, mostly," said the cook.

"Treacle," said a sleepy voice behind her.

"Collar that Dormouse," the Queen shrieked out. "Behead that Dormouse! Turn that Dormouse out of court! Pinch him! Off with his whiskers!"

For a few moments, the whole court was in confusion, getting the Dormouse turned out. By

the time they had settled down again, the cook had disappeared.

"Never mind!" said the King, with an air of great relief. "Call the next witness."

And he added in an undertone to the Queen, "Really, my dear, YOU must cross-examine the next witness. It quite makes my forehead ache!"

Alice watched the White Rabbit as he fumbled over the list, feeling very curious to see what the next witness would be like.

Imagine her surprise, when the White Rabbit read out, at the top of his shrill little voice, the name 'Alice!'

CHAPTER 12

Alice's Evidence

Here!" cried Alice, jumping up. She quite forgot in the flurry of the moment, how large she had grown in the last few minutes; and she jumped up in such a hurry that she tipped over the jury-box with the hem of her skirt. As a result, all the jurymen tumbled down on to the heads of the crowd below, and there they lay sprawling about.

"Oh, I BEG your pardon!" she exclaimed in a tone of great dismay, and began picking them up as quickly as she could.

"The trial cannot proceed," said the King in a very grave voice, "until all the jurymen are back in their proper places... ALL," he repeated with great emphasis, staring hard at Alice as he said so.

Alice looked at the jury-box, and saw that, in her haste, she had put the Lizard in head downwards! The poor little thing was waving its tail about in melancholy, being quite unable to move. Alice soon got it out again, and put it right.

As soon as the jury had recovered a bit from the shock of being upset, and their slates and pencils had been found, they set to work very diligently to write out a history of the accident.

"What do you know about this business?" the King asked Alice.

"Nothing," said Alice.

"Nothing WHATEVER?" persisted the King.

"Nothing whatever," said Alice.

"That's very important," the King said, turning to the jury. They were just beginning to write this down on their slates, when the White Rabbit interrupted, "UNimportant, your Majesty means, of course," he said in a very respectful tone, but frowning and making faces at him as he spoke.

"UNimportant, of course, I meant," the King hastily said, and went on to himself in an undertone, 'important–unimportant– unimportant–important–' as if he were trying which word sounded best.

Some of the jury wrote it down 'important', and some 'unimportant'.

Alice could see this, as she was near enough to look over their slates; 'but it doesn't matter a bit,' she thought to herself.

At this moment, the King, who had been for

some time busily writing in his note-book, cackled out, 'Silence!' and read out from his book, 'Rule Forty-two: ALL PERSONS MORE THAN A MILE HIGH TO LEAVE THE COURT.' Everybody looked at Alice.

"I'M not a mile high," said Alice.

"You are," said the King.

"Nearly two miles high," added the Queen.

"Well, I shall not go, at any rate," said Alice, "besides, that's not a regular rule. You invented it just now."

"It's the oldest rule in the book," said the King. "Then it ought to be Number One," said Alice. The King turned pale, and shut his note-book hastily.

"Consider your verdict," he said to the jury, in a low, trembling voice.

"There's more evidence to come yet, please your Majesty," said the White Rabbit, jumping up in a great hurry; "this paper has just been picked up."

"What's in it?" said the Queen.

"I haven't opened it yet," said the White Rabbit, "but it seems to be a letter, written by the prisoner to–to somebody."

"It must have been that," said the King, "unless it was written to nobody, which isn't usual, you know."

"Who is it directed to?" said one of the jurymen.

"It isn't directed at all," said the White Rabbit; "in fact, there's nothing written on the OUTSIDE."

He unfolded the paper as he spoke, and added 'It isn't a letter, after all. It's a set of verses.'

"Are they in the prisoner's handwriting?" asked another of they jurymen.

"No, they're not," said the White Rabbit, "and that's the queerest thing about it." (The jury all looked puzzled.)

"He must have imitated somebody else's

hand," said the King. (The jury all brightened up again.)

"Please your Majesty," said the Knave, "I didn't write it, and they can't prove I did. There's no name signed at the end."

"If you didn't sign it," said the King, "that only makes the matter worse. You MUST have meant some mischief, or else you'd have signed your name like an honest man."

There was a general clapping of hands at this. It was the first really clever thing the King had said that day.

"That PROVES his guilt," said the Queen. "It proves nothing of the sort!" said Alice. "Why, you don't even know what they're about!"

"Read them," said the King.

The White Rabbit put on his spectacles. "Where shall I begin, please your Majesty?" he asked.

"Begin at the beginning," the King said gravely, "and go on till you come to the end. Then

stop." These were the verses the White Rabbit
read:--

> 'They told me you had been to her,
> And mentioned me to him:
> She gave me a good character,
> But said I could not swim.
>
> He sent them word I had not gone
> (We know it to be true):
> If she should push the matter on,
> What would become of you?
>
> I gave her one, they gave him two,
> You gave us three or more;
> They all returned from him to you,
> Though they were mine before.
>
> If I or she should chance to be
> Involved in this affair,
> He trusts to you to set them free,
> Exactly as we were.
>
> My notion was that you had been
> (Before she had this fit)
> An obstacle that came between

Him, and ourselves, and it.
Don't let him know she liked them best,
For this must ever be
A secret, kept from all the rest,
Between yourself and me.'

"That's the most important piece of evidence we've heard yet," said the King, rubbing his hands. "So now let the jury—"

"If any one of them can explain it," said Alice, (she had grown so large in the last few minutes that she wasn't a bit afraid of interrupting him,) "I'll give him sixpence. I don't believe there's an atom of meaning in it."

The jury all wrote down on their slates, 'SHE doesn't believe there's an atom of meaning in it,' but none of them attempted to explain the paper.

"If there's no meaning in it," said the King, "that saves a world of trouble, you know, as we needn't try to find any. And yet I don't know," he went on, spreading out the verses on his knee, and looking at them with one eye; "I seem to see some meaning in them, after all.

'–SAID I COULD NOT SWIM—'

"You can't swim, can you?" he added, turning to the Knave.

The Knave shook his head sadly. "Do I look like it?' he said. (Which he certainly did NOT, being made entirely of cardboard.)

"All right, so far," said the King, and he went on muttering over the verses to himself, '"WE KNOW IT TO BE TRUE—' that's the jury, of course—'I GAVE HER ONE, THEY GAVE HIM TWO—' why, that must be what he did with the tarts, you know—"

"But, it goes on 'THEY ALL RETURNED FROM HIM TO YOU,'" said Alice.

"Why, there they are!" said the King triumphantly, pointing to the tarts on the table. "Nothing can be clearer than THAT. Then again—

'BEFORE SHE HAD THIS FIT...' you never

had fits, my dear, I think?" he said to the Queen.

"Never!" said the Queen furiously, throwing an inkstand at the Lizard as she spoke.

"Then the words don't FIT you," said the King, looking round the court with a smile. There was a dead silence.

"It's a pun!" the King added in an offended tone, and everybody laughed, "Let the jury consider their verdict," the King said, for about the twentieth time that day.

"No, no!" said the Queen. "Sentence first—verdict afterwards."

"The idea of having the sentence first, is nonsense!" said Alice, loudly.

"Hold your tongue!" said the Queen, turning purple. "I won't!" said Alice.

"Off with her head!" the Queen shouted at the top of her voice. Nobody moved.

"Who cares for you?" said Alice, (she had grown to her full size by this time.) "You're nothing but a pack of cards!"

At this the whole pack rose up into the air, and came flying down upon her. Alice gave a little scream, half of fright and half of anger, and tried to beat them off, and found herself....
....lying on the bank, with her head in the lap of her sister, who was gently brushing away some dead leaves that had fluttered down from the trees upon her face.

"Wake up, Alice dear!" said her sister; "Why, what a long sleep you've had!"

"Oh, I've had such a curious dream!" said Alice, and she told her sister, as well as she could remember them, all these strange adventures of hers that you have just been reading about.

When Alice had finished, her sister kissed her, and said, "It WAS a curious dream, dear, certainly. But now run in for your tea; it's getting late."

So Alice got up and ran off, thinking while she ran, about the wonderful dream that she had. But her sister sat still just as she left her, leaning her head on her hand, watching the setting sun, and thinking of little Alice and all her wonderful Adventures. Soon, she too began dreaming, and this was her dream:–

First, she dreamed of little Alice herself, and once again the tiny hands were clasped upon her knee, and the bright eager eyes were looking up into hers. She could hear her voice, and see that queer little toss of her head to keep back the wandering hair that WOULD always get into her eyes. And still as she listened, or seemed to listen, the whole place around her became alive the strange creatures of her little sister's dream.

The long grass rustled at her feet as the White Rabbit hurried by. The frightened Mouse splashed his way through the neighboring pool.

She could hear the rattle of the teacups as the March Hare and his friends shared their never-ending meal, and the shrill voice of the

Queen ordering off her unfortunate guests to execution. Once more the pig-baby was sneezing on the Duchess's knee, while plates and dishes crashed around it; once more the shriek of the Gryphon, the squeaking of the Lizard's slate-pencil, and the choking of the suppressed guinea-pigs, filled the air, mixed up with the distant sobs of the miserable Mock Turtle.

So she sat on, with closed eyes, and half believed herself in Wonderland, though she knew she had but to open them again, and all would change to dull reality. The grass would be only rustling in the wind; and the pool rippling to the waving of the reeds; the rattling teacups would change to tinkling sheep-bells; and the Queen's shrill cries to the voice of the shepherd boy; and the sneeze of the baby, the shriek of the Gryphon, and all the other queer noises, would change (she knew) to the confused clamor of the busy farmyard; while the lowing of the cattle in the distance would take the place